ballykissangel™
behind the scenes

ballykissangel™
behind the scenes

GEOFF TIBBALLS

HEADLINE

ACKNOWLEDGEMENTS

The author would like to thank the cast and crew of *Ballykissangel* and the people of Avoca for their friendly cooperation in the preparation of this book. Special thanks to Chris Griffin and Kate Bowe. Thanks also to Tony Garnett, Mike Watts and Chris Harries at World Productions, Jamie Munro and Julie Cullingworth at BBC Television, Suzanne Ross-Bain, Roxy Spencer, and Heather Holden-Brown and Lorraine Jerram at Headline.

Photographs © 1997 BBC and World Productions Ltd, except for the following:
    Bord Failte–Irish Tourist Board: pp.116-17
    The Slide File: pp. 10-11, 20-21, 30-31, 70-71, 76-7, 82-3, 110-11, 117, 119

First published in 1997
by HEADLINE BOOK PUBLISHING

10 9 8 7 6 5 4 3 2 1

British Library Cataloguing in Publication Data
Tibballs, Geoff
    Ballykissangel : behind the scenes
    1. Ballykissangel (Television program)
    I. Title
    791.4'572

    ISBN 0 7472 2106 5

Printed and bound in Italy by Canale & C.Spa.

HEADLINE BOOK PUBLISHING
A division of Hodder Headline PLC
338 Euston Road
London NW1 3BH

Contents

INTRODUCTION

To the viewing nation, *Ballykissangel* has been a breath of fresh air. No blatant sex, no violence, no strong police presence – just a good wholesome story about the enchanting characters of a peaceful rural community in picturesque Ireland. It quickly proved to be exactly what Sunday evenings were made for, the first series attracting an average audience of 14.5 million, making it the BBC's highest-rated weekly drama for over fifteen years. Such was the BBC's confidence that a second series was commissioned even before the first episode had been screened. Their faith has been rewarded with the show continuing to earn high ratings as well as the Royal Television Society Award for Best Drama.

Father Peter Clifford soon settled into life in Ballykissangel and was enlisted to help bar owner Assumpta Fitzgerald in the urgent relocation of several crates of beer and boxes of crisps.

Yet behind the idyllic pictures lies a tragic story. For Joy Lale, producer of that first series, was killed in a car crash in Ireland shortly before the end of filming. The unenviable task of succeeding her has fallen to Chris Griffin, an award-winning producer with over twenty years' experience and with an impressive list of credits including *The Long Good Friday, Max Headroom, First Love, Yesterday's Dreams, The Zero Option* and *Preston Front*.

Chris Griffin recalls: 'I was on my way towards finishing *Preston Front* when I got a phone call asking me to go and see Tony Garnett of World Productions. He explained the tragic situation and said that he needed somebody to take over. Naturally before committing myself to *Ballykissangel*, I wanted to read the scripts from the first series and I found that an enlightening experience. They had such humour and reflected Ireland in a way in which I don't think we'd been used to seeing it on television in recent years. Then I saw the fine cuts and really became involved from there in post-production.

'At that stage, we didn't know whether it would be a success or not so the BBC suggested we do a little audience research exercise where a cross-section of the public were invited to watch the first episode at a special screening. We did two in London, two in Birmingham and two in Manchester. I went along to one in London and one in Birmingham and sat anonymously at the back. The feedback

OPPOSITE Cast members pictured beside the bridge at Avoca, County Wicklow, the real-life Ballykissangel.

Producer Chris Griffin.

from the public was quite extraordinary. Everyone was extremely enthusiastic. The very fact that it was a young English priest going to work in Ireland had instant appeal. They warmed to the characters even though they didn't recognise many of the actors other than Stephen Tompkinson and Tony Doyle, which was good because it meant they believed in the characters. In particular they liked Quigley, in whom they saw echoes of Arthur Daley.

'I had been dying to ask them a question and eventually at the end of the exercise I said: "On a score of one to ten, what would you give this series?" Almost without exception, they gave eight or more and the majority were nines or tens. About the only dissenting voice was a guy who didn't like anything to do with Ireland or the Irish and gave it a four.

'As I took over as producer for the second and third series, one thing that worried me was the reaction of the Irish people – you know the sort of thing, here's this bunch of Englishmen making a film about Ireland and it's all going to be clichéd with leprechauns and "Oirishness". But nobody has ever accused us of that. The only character who is anywhere near a cliché is Eamonn, the old hill farmer, but every Irish person I've met says they know someone just like Eamonn. I think it's refreshing to show an image of Ireland that is not necessarily newsworthy but is real.

'There are no belly laughs in *Ballykissangel*. All of the comedy comes out of the characters and the way they are portrayed. But it's got a lot of charm and people can identify with it. And to my mind the star of the show is Ballykissangel itself, rather than any individual.

'We've always been concerned about the development of the relationship between Father Clifford and Assumpta. Some people have said they should end up together while the rest of the population have said, "on no account". If they did, I think it would be the end for both characters. True, it's been difficult keeping that sexual tension going without becoming repetitive but we've managed it so far. And really what we're aiming for is a community piece because even the smaller characters in *Ballykissangel* are excellent and that includes those who only come in for an episode or two.

'It has been an absolute joy to work in Ireland and the people of Avoca, the real-life Ballykissangel, have been incredibly cooperative and welcoming. As a producer, you tend to think that for the first year you can get away with using a particular location for weeks on end; by the second year, the novelty can wear off; and by the third year, you'd normally anticipate plenty of problems. But here it's been wonderful. And I like to think that we have been good for Avoca because, as a result of *Ballykissangel,* Avoca has been able to obtain EU grants in case visitors are disappointed that there's not enough of Ballykissangel in the village.

'The only problem is that they are doing up the village to the point where it worries me a little bit with continuity. I thought the first block of filming we'd do would be mid-May and we'd come back in July to find the road had been re-laid and the houses re-painted! So we had to go along and say, "Look, please don't change anything until we've finished."

'Filming in England can be a bit of a trial sometimes, but the Irish police, the Garda, are so willing. I think it's all about the Irish attitude and the pace of life. For example I've never come across any road rage here. I remember one of my first trips to Ireland was on a recce and our minibus stopped in the middle of the road because something was coming the other way. The two drivers had a conversation for the best part of a minute, yet, in contrast to what would have happened in England, nobody behind sounded a horn. When I mentioned this to one of the locals, he said: "Ah well, they probably had something important to say to each other." That's Ireland…and I love it.'

A close encounter outside Fitzgerald's for Padraig O'Kelly, Siobhan Mehigan, Father Clifford, Assumpta and Dr Michael Ryan.

CHAPTER ONE

The Birth of Ballykissangel

For a series set amid so much Irish greenery, it is somewhat ironic that *Ballykissangel* started out on an oil rig in the North Sea. It is the brainchild of former sports journalist and *That's Life* presenter Kieran Prendiville who, at the moment of conception, was penning *Roughnecks,* his successful BBC drama about life on a North Sea oil rig.

He explains: 'I was writing *Roughnecks* and had got as far as episode four when the BBC announced that it had overspent its annual budget by millions of pounds, as a result of which a number of projects were being cancelled. I knew that *Roughnecks* would be expensive and I honestly thought I was going to lose it. Also, *Roughnecks* was quite dark, deep and claustrophobic by nature and I'd spent a fair bit of time on oil rigs in the North Sea, just outside the Arctic Circle. So I was desperately trying to go somewhere away from the clatter of machinery and the smell of diesel oil, to a place where the air was clean and the sky was blue. I found myself regressing into childhood to places where my father used to take us on summer holidays. He was born and raised at Killorglin, near Ballykissanne in County Kerry. So while I was on the rig, I started imagining this place and the people who lived there as a way of getting off the rig and then when I thought I was going to lose *Roughnecks,* I started dreaming up some characters.

'I did ten pages of detailed biographies. What I really wanted to do was explore the collision between people's ideas and expectations of rural Ireland and the reality. Rural Ireland to me now is a place where Rupert Murdoch speaks to as many people as the Pope and I thought that had a lot of comic potential. That's the heart of the whole series. And that's why it's so important that the central character is an outsider so that we can explore Ballykissangel through his eyes. The point about Peter is not that he's a priest but that he's an outsider, and I needed some kind of job that would bring him into the heart of the community and affect the community by virtue of what he did. He could have been a doctor or a lawyer, but the more I thought about it, he had to be a priest…and an English priest at that, so that he would be even more of a fish out of water.'

The sexual tension between the priest and the bar owner has been an ongoing theme in Ballykissangel. They came perilously close to kissing during rehearsals for Padraig and Brendan's play.

Not only was Kieran Prendiville attracted by the outsider element of an English priest and by the interesting nature of his work but, as a second-generation Irishman himself, he was only too aware that the three focal points of any Irish village are the church, the pub and the shop. Thus all three featured prominently in his list of characters, along with other rural regulars such as the vet (Siobhan), the Gard (Ambrose), the schoolteacher (Brendan), the doctor (Dr Ryan) and the entrepreneur (Quigley). To capitalise on the relationships between the various characters, Kieran Prendiville created the sexual tension between the young priest and the beautiful bar owner and arranged for the scrupulously honest Gard to be engaged to the roguish businessman's daughter.

'The forbidden love between Peter and Assumpta is a very powerful, dramatic theme. In my mind, there was a pyramid with Peter as the central character, Assumpta as the central female character, then Quigley and so on down.

'Peter has his expectations confounded all the time. He comes from an inner city parish in Manchester, quite expecting that when he goes to rural Ireland, everyone will go round tipping their caps to him, saying, "Morning, Father", "How are you, Father?" and all that. But the first thing he finds is that the local publican can't stand the clergy. Great start! Another example of this collision between expectation and reality is when Peter arrives and thinks life will be conducted at a snail's pace, but gets a bawling-out from Father Mac because his only transport is a mountain bike. Father Mac tells him mountains are designed for goats, not bikes, so he should get a car. *Ballykissangel* constantly reflects this image.

'It's presumptuous of me to write about rural Ireland from an office in Hammersmith, West London, which is another reason why it is essential that we discover the place through the priest's eyes. Having said that, I have been going backwards and forwards to Ireland for as long as I've lived. And at Hammersmith tube station you can buy every Irish provincial newspaper so I used to trawl those every week for goings-on in rural Ireland and distil the best stories and see if I could work them in some way to turn them into fiction. The papers have been the source of quite a few ideas. For example, I read about an annual slave auction in Kerry and I was able to incorporate that into *Ballykissangel*. Puck Fair is another Kerry ceremony where they put a goat up on a platform. We used a ram. And in an episode of the third series there's a food festival where everyone in BallyK cooks something to raise money for charity. Again, that's real.'

Kieran Prendiville emphasises that although Father Clifford is the principal character, the rest of the community have always been a vital part of the show's planning. 'I was determined to call it *Ballykissangel* and not something like *Peter's Travels* because it was an ensemble piece about the people of the town. You have to explore the other characters.

'Although the name Ballykissangel is adapted from Ballykissanne, it actually means in Gaelic, "The town of the banished angel", which sums up Peter's predicament quite nicely. I had always set the series in County Kerry but from my experience in television, I knew there was no way it could be filmed in Kerry because of financial considerations. It would be too far to travel from a Dublin base. But when I was formulating the original idea, I had to have somewhere in my mind and I thought of Glenbeigh, a small town in Kerry near Dingle Bay, which had a big wide street and a church up a little hill. I knew we'd never shoot it there and, to be honest, it was too close to home anyway. I didn't want people my family know recognising themselves and taking offence at being called the local chancer like Quigley. And eventually we ended up with Avoca which has been ideal.'

Born in Oldham, Lancashire, Kieran Prendiville began work as a copy boy at the Oldham Press Agency – 'making tea, getting shouted at and covering Oldham Athletic. I then went to Fleet Street for three years as an agency reporter, doing news, sport and crime stories. From there I joined the BBC as a researcher on *Nationwide* and *Man Alive* before being attached to a new consumer programme called *That's Life*. I was a researcher on the first series where Esther Rantzen's team on screen were Bob Wellings and George Layton. That didn't work out so they decided to put the researchers on screen, the way they had done in *Braden's Week* with Esther and John Pitman. The idea of going on live TV was good for my ego but I stayed longer than I should have done. I remember a moment of blinding clarity. I was holding up some stupid vegetable and I had this voice in my head saying, "you know, you look more like a pr**k than that parsnip – you've got to get out." I never felt comfortable doing the show – I didn't enjoy it. I always felt more nervous inside than I thought was natural.

'After *That's Life*, I did *Nationwide*, *Tomorrow's World* and *Grandstand*. Where I worked at the BBC in Kensington House, you had the arts and features department, the science and features department and sport, and we all used the same bar. So I used to say to the sports guys: "Give us a job." And I kept asking until they put me on *Grandstand*, doing live football match reports at the final whistle. Sport was the only thing I knew about. I knew nothing about science and had to learn about it for *Tomorrow's World*. But some of those match reports could be hairy. I remember we'd been warned by the editor that if we went over thirty seconds, we'd never work for the BBC again. And I could hear Des Lynam in the studio saying, "And now over to Elland Road" just as the sixth goal went in. I knew it would take me thirty seconds just to list the scorers. To make matters worse, my notes were everywhere and people were climbing all over me. It was a nightmare.

'I also covered the 1984 Los Angeles Olympics and went over to Ireland to do a film on Irish racing. And I did a series of religious documentaries called *The Human Factor* which went out on a Sunday lunchtime at noon. It was such an obscure time that even my mother didn't watch it!

'It seemed to me that I'd run out of programmes and because I'd always wanted to write, on my fortieth birthday I said, "I'm going to do it." The first things I did were episodes of *Boon* and then I wrote for *The Bill* for two years, *Perfect Scoundrels*, *Roughnecks* and now *Ballykissangel*.'

Filming in the main street of Avoca.

It was in 1992 that Kieran Prendiville sent his outline for *Ballykissangel* to his agent Julia Kreitman, although he admits candidly: 'I honestly didn't expect anyone to be interested in it.' But Julia Kreitman knew of a joint initiative between BBC Northern Ireland and the Republic station RTE to encourage Irish writing and she got in touch with Roxy Spencer, a script editor at BBC Northern Ireland, and who would go on to become script editor on the first series of *Ballykissangel*.

'I was looking for a series set in Ireland,' remembers Roxy, 'when Julia Kreitman sent me Kieran's treatment for *Ballykissangel*. I immediately loved it and went to Robert

The conventional romance between Ambrose and Niamh Egan has provided a neat contrast to the forbidden relationship between Father Clifford and Assumpta.

Cooper, the Head of BBC Northern Ireland, and said, "We should do this." He was equally impressed but BBC Northern Ireland had no background of producing long-running series. It so happened that Robert had been involved in meetings with Tony Garnett of World Productions, a company with an outstanding drama pedigree including *Between the Lines, Cardiac Arrest* and more recently *This Life*. And, of course, Tony is one of the most distinguished names in television, dating back to *Cathy Come Home, Days of Hope* and *Law and Order*. Tony thought it was different from anything else around at the time and so World took it up. When it was first commissioned, it was to be a joint venture between the BBC and RTE, but RTE then dropped out. They've since shown *Ballykissangel* but they've had to pay for it!

'It was then a matter of getting the green light from the controllers and happily Nick Elliott, who had just been appointed BBC head of drama, made *Ballykissangel* one of his first commissions in September 1994. Less than nine months later, we started filming. Ironically, Nick, who was so supportive, has now returned to ITV and is therefore up against his "baby".

'By then Joy Lale, who had worked with Tony Garnett on *Between the Lines* and who had an excellent knowledge of what makes successful Sunday evening drama, having been script editor on *All Creatures Great and Small*, had joined as producer. One of our main jobs was to trim the number of characters. Kieran originally had twenty-one characters, including a Dutch clockmender and an Irish playwright. And Quigley had three daughters. We thought this was too many for the audience to take in with only six establishing episodes and so we set about combining some and losing others altogether. Father Mac was going to have a housekeeper but we were worried about the clichés of Irish priests' housekeepers (and this was before *Father Ted*!) so instead we gave many of her qualities to the shopkeeper

Kathleen. Even at a very late stage, we lost two more bar room characters. But by reducing the numbers we were able to concentrate more on the parallel relationships between Peter and Assumpta and Ambrose and Niamh, the one forbidden, the other perfectly natural, which made for a good contrast.'

Tony Garnett recalls: 'I knew of Kieran Prendiville's work from *Roughnecks* and when he first gave me the one-liner about an English priest going to work in a village in rural Ireland, I said, "Great. A classic fish out of water situation." It reminded me of *Northern Exposure*. We went on to develop it fifty-fifty with BBC Northern Ireland and I brought in Joy Lale as producer. After Nick Elliott had given us the go-ahead, certain people at the BBC objected to the title, claiming that nobody could even say "Ballykissangel". But I knew it needed a distinctive title and that it also had to be the name of the place since the series was very much about the community. Kieran and Joy felt the same way, so we stuck to our guns.

'We also encountered considerable opposition in various parts of the BBC over casting Stephen Tompkinson as the priest. We were looking for someone who could be funny, compassionate, appealing and believable as a priest. We saw a lot of actors but we were convinced that Stephen was the right man for the part. But certain executives, never having worked in drama, are naturally experts on casting! Again we won the day and I think it's fair to say our decision has been thoroughly vindicated.

'Dervla Kirwan was very much Joy's idea – and again she has been magnificent – while Tony Doyle worked with me on *Between the Lines* and was just a natural for our "JR". Tony's a great actor. And we were really lucky to get so many talented Irish actors in the other roles.

'People ask me why *Ballykissangel* has proved so popular and I think it's down to the show's sense of community. These days so much of society is isolated – there isn't that sense of fellowship and looking after your neighbours. Whereas in Ballykissangel, although they may have their squabbles, they all rally round if anyone is in trouble. Take the episode which began with Kathleen's house on fire. Now she's not a particularly sympathetic character but everyone, even Quigley, rallied round with chains of buckets and then repaired the damage. For me, that story was the soul of *Ballykissangel*.'

'When you write a TV drama,' says Kieran Prendiville, 'you're never really sure that it's going to happen because it takes so long to get on to the screen. Even when they say it's going to happen, there's always some part of you that thinks it's all going to go horribly wrong. So the most exciting thing for me was going to Avoca for the first time and seeing a little tea shop which the crew had converted into a post office. Over the top, it had "Ballykissangel" in white letters on a green background and I thought, "Wow! It's real. It's actually happening."

'I would say that I've enjoyed *Ballykissangel* more than anything I have ever written. Unusually, the writing process itself has been a real joy and it has been tremendous working first with Tony Garnett and Joy Lale and now Brenda Reid and Chris Griffin.

'I confess to being delighted but bemused by its success,' adds Kieran, whose brother Paddy edits the Irish satirical magazine *Phoenix*. His other brother is a professor of obstetrics and gynaecology at a Dublin hospital. 'Somehow it's struck a chord. Maybe it's because you know there won't be any muggings, shootings, stabbings or bad language in *Ballykissangel*. It wasn't a conscious effort though, and I didn't find it in any way restrictive not to write those things. Quite simply, they were things which wouldn't happen there. In a way I hope I never do find out the secret of its success because I'm sure I'd try and do the same thing again and fail.'

Kieran, who was an altar boy in his early years, is aware that he hasn't tackled some of the more contentious issues to do with the clergy. 'There's really no message,' he insists. 'I just wanted it to be funny. The clergy like the show because they've had so much appalling publicity in Ireland so it's something of a relief for them not to see a priest with his hands in the till or his trousers round his ankles. But I don't think I'm being untruthful – there are plenty of dedicated, decent priests and Father Clifford happens to be one of them. I wish I'd met more of them when I was a kid!

'No one would call me a devout Catholic so I had to do a fair amount of research. But in none of my scripts do I show too much detail of the life of a priest. I've shown a few confessional scenes because to most people that is the most interesting aspect of being a Catholic priest, and to an outsider it's bizarre and extraordinary. I find it bizarre and extraordinary, and I was brought up as a Catholic…'

Kieran Prendiville is one of eight writers on the third series of *Ballykissangel*. Among the others is former *EastEnders* writer Rio Fanning who also scripted two episodes for the second series. Rio, who has homes in Northamptonshire and at Annascaul on the Dingle Peninsula in the West of Ireland, grew up in the Irish market town of Tralee. 'It was only a two-minute walk into the country so I am more than familiar with the rural setting of BallyK. In fact, BallyK is a heaving metropolis compared to Annascaul. I find it useful to go over there whenever I'm writing an episode of *Ballykissangel* so that I can soak up the atmosphere and get back on the right wavelength. The rhythm of the language and the expressions people use are so different from Northamptonshire. If you go into any pub in rural Kerry, you hear the same conversations as you would in BallyK.

'The brief all writers on the series are given is to avoid stereotypical Irish. The aim is to provide laughter and tears, solid dramatic stories, romance and zany situations which are only just on this side of credulity, but definitely no begorrahs, shillelaghs or Little People. Being part of a team of writers on a series is rather like being in the team for a relay race. You pick up the baton from the writer of the previous episode and try to progress smoothly before handing over to the next writer, preferably without tripping anyone else up.

'I particularly like writing for Quigley. I've known Tony Doyle for thirty years since we acted together at Stratford East in a series of Irish plays. I still remember Bernard Levin's review in the *Daily Mail*: "This season of Irish comedy at Stratford East is rapidly becoming no laughing matter…" Tony and I have worked together on quite a few occasions since, so writing for him is a bit like writing for myself. I did actually write a part for myself in the second series – Quigley's old enemy Mossy Phelan – but they wouldn't give it to me.

Director Dermot Boyd talks over a scene with Niall Toibin who plays Father Mac, the embodiment of the traditional Irish Catholic priest.

'I still act occasionally and envy the warm reception which the cast of *Ballykissangel* get from the public. I remember being in an episode of *Z Cars* in which I played a thug who hit a policeman. The next night I was set upon in a pub in Farnham by a gang shouting: "Now let's see how tough you are." It can be tough when fact and fiction collide.'

Never were the laughter and tears which are the staple diet of *Ballykissangel* more evident than in the last few days of filming the first series. Stephen Tompkinson remembers a massive party for cast, crew and villagers at Avoca. 'They closed the whole village down, there were about eight hundred people outside the bar which doubles as Fitzgerald's and three Irish bands on an open-topped lorry. It was a real hoot.'

Then a couple of days later Joy Lale was killed in a car crash on a country road while returning from filming one night. 'Everyone was devastated,' says Stephen. 'Joy had actually learned to drive in Ireland so that she wouldn't need to have a driver on the production. She and her husband had just bought a place in Ireland and were planning to settle there. The people of Avoca felt responsible in some way that this had happened on their territory, so we held a Mass for them. The church was absolutely heaving with people. We all felt that we had to finish the series for Joy's sake, to do it justice for all the work she had put into it.'

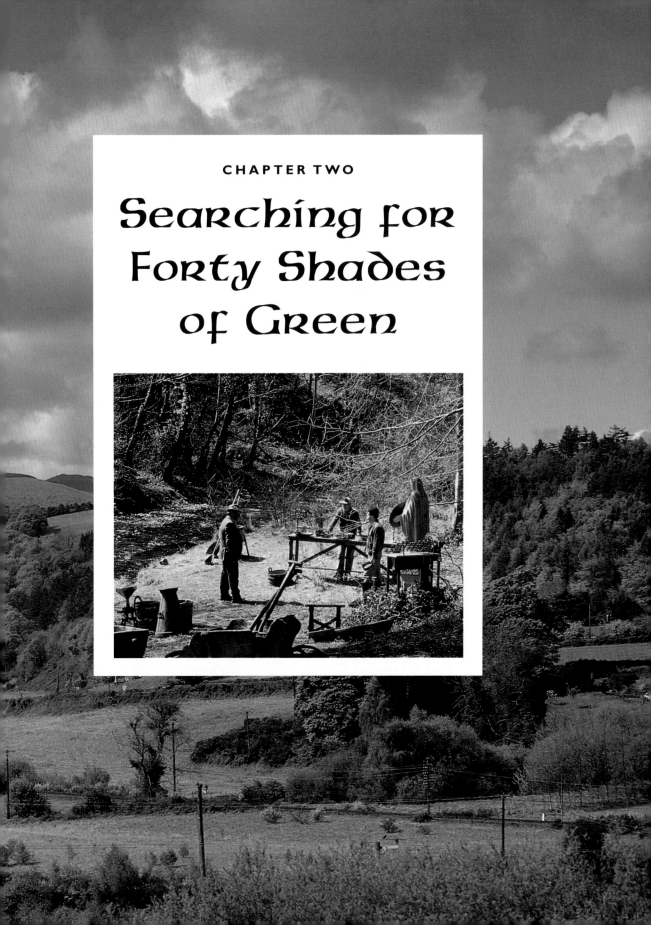

CHAPTER TWO

Searching for Forty Shades of Green

ASSUMPTA: *Forty shades of green! Forty shades of grey*
would be more accurate, but there's the image to think of.

Assumpta (Dervla Kirwan)
on the studio set of
Fitzgerald's. Note the old
map of Wicklow on the wall.

PREVIOUS PAGE *The Avoca*
River provides a perfect
backdrop for Liam and
Donal's shrine to Our Lady
of the Motherlode.

The first and biggest task facing Joy Lale and the production crew back in early 1995 was finding an Irish village to play Ballykissangel. Although series creator Kieran Prendiville had conjured up visions of County Kerry on the west coast, County Wicklow was the preferred venue because of its proximity to Dublin and its vast diversity of scenery. So Constance Harris, the location manager on the first series, scoured the mountains and valleys of Wicklow in search of somewhere suitable. She visited as many as thirty villages, carefully noting the pros and cons of each one before preparing a shortlist for Joy Lale. Among the villages on that list was Avoca, a dozen or so miles inland from Wicklow Town.

Chris Griffin says: 'Apparently Joy took one look at the bridge, the pub opposite and the dominant church on the hill and decided that Avoca was the place to film. Without being disrespectful, looking at the layout of the village, I would have foreseen the nightmare which has happened. We jokingly call the junction by the bridge and the pub "the crossroads from hell" because of the volume of traffic. But if I hadn't chosen Avoca, I would have made a mistake because it really is a wonderful setting. I know we have to cope with the coachloads of tourists who pour in to the village to see where *Ballykissangel* is filmed, but we're really just victims of our own success.'

The directors on the first series were Richard Standeven and Paul Harrison. 'By the time Richard and I arrived in Ireland in February,' says Paul Harrison, 'Joy had already settled happily on Avoca. It was a very cold, wet dark February day and the first time I saw the place, I hated it because it wasn't what we were expecting and it wasn't how it was written. Avoca is a linear village – straight up and down – whereas the way Kieran Prendiville had written the piece, you came out of the pub and went to the shop and then you came out of the shop and went to the church. It was a traditional square.

'But it took no time at all for Richard and I to fall in love with the place. At first I had thought I could never shoot it but as soon as we started filming, it all just fell into place. What Joy had wanted was a beautiful rural backdrop with a village in the middle, but then you'd walk down the street and there'd be a satellite dish – a mixture of the 1990s and an old-fashioned rural community. Avoca had all of these things plus the three essentials – the church, the pub and the shop – which are the centre of all communities.'

The geographical differences between the fictional Ballykissangel and the real Avoca necessitated a hasty rewrite of the scripts. Kieran Prendiville says: 'Joy Lale drew me a map of Avoca on the back of a Post-It note and asked me to take it away and marry it up to the script. I didn't get to visit Avoca until we were well into shooting. I remember it was a beautiful sunny day and my heart soared. It was just a wonderful setting.'

Although the production team were delighted with their Ballykissangel, there remained the small matter of whether the villagers of Avoca would be equally overjoyed about the prospect of having an eighty-strong film crew camping on their doorstep for most of the summer. To film without the cooperation of the locals would have been impossible and so Joy Lale, Constance Harris and Richard Standeven chaired a public meeting in Avoca to outline their proposals. Most of the villagers attended, among them the priest of Avoca, Father Dan Breen. He

The setting of the dominant church above the river was one of the reasons why the village of Avoca caught the imagination of the late Joy Lale, producer of the first series.

remembers: 'Joy Lale and Richard Standeven said what they intended to do and asked whether they would be welcome. They didn't pull any punches – they didn't try and pretend that everything would be rosy. And I think we all respected them for that. But what really clinched it was when the meeting ended, they said: "There's an open bar down the road." There was a free bar for an hour, then it was extended an hour, then another hour. They like a drink round here and so they all staggered home happy.'

Now that the people of Avoca had given their blessing, serious planning could get under way. However, the idea of filming solely in Avoca was quickly scuppered by economics. Paul Harrison explains: 'We had originally hoped to shoot virtually everything there because you could stand at the church and see Quigley's house, Siobhan's house, the lot. But economics dictated that we had to be in Dublin because for a crew to film in Avoca requires overnight stays. And they work out extremely expensive.

'So for the first series we built sets for Fitzgerald's and Father Clifford's house in a warehouse near Dublin. We have subsequently taken those sets and other interiors to Ardmore Studios at Bray. We have never filmed any interiors at the Fountain Bar in Avoca, which doubles as Fitzgerald's, only exteriors. You will see Quigley, or whoever, walk through the door of the real bar and straight into the studio replica. The only interiors we now use in Avoca are Hendley's shop and the church, although we did use the school for a couple of episodes in series two. The rest is either in the studio or around Dublin. For example, Quigley's house and Father Mac's are both up at Enniskerry, which is much nearer to Dublin. Some houses are in two locations. The exterior of Ambrose's house is a guest house in Avoca, but the interior is a house at Enniskerry. Nothing is quite what it seems in *Ballykissangel* – half of the exterior of Father Clifford's house is now a cake shop!

'We do try and keep disruption in Avoca to a minimum and the only real problem is the traffic at the crossroads. That wasn't a problem filming the first series because people didn't know about *Ballykissangel*. Although it's a quiet village, there are a lot of fans here and unfortunately there is only one small road through Avoca and that runs along the main street, over the bridge and out on to the main road on the other side. So wherever we are filming – Fitzgerald's, Hendley's, the church – we get all of the traffic, tourist coaches and all, passing by.

'The trouble is, there is nowhere to hide in Avoca – there are no back lanes. You can't get out of the back of most of the houses to film because the mountain is right up against the wall. So we've had to create lanes and expand the village by shooting in Enniskerry. Whenever a character is supposed to be walking behind a house or going between unspecified houses, we have to film that scene in Enniskerry.

'Luckily the Gards in Avoca are terrific and they work with us all the time. I remember doing a set-up for a huge fair up on the car park opposite the church and I was discussing the shot with my assistant director. We were there for about forty minutes and then a voice came through my radio: "Can I let these people go now?" The Gard had held up the traffic for forty minutes, and there was no complaint, no fuss, no problem. Everyone in Ireland has a much more laid-back attitude.

'The one thing we have had to do is stop the villagers smartening up Avoca too much, because it wrecks our continuity. All of the telegraph cables and electricity wires in the area were due to go underground in the summer of 1997 but our location manager, Luke Johnston, managed to persuade the council to leave them above ground for the time being. They have built a small park area opposite Fitzgerald's with EU money, which is great for the village but unfortunately it opens up a view of council houses which doesn't really suit us. They also knocked down an old house next to the park and that opened up much too large a vista on that side of the street. So in its place we had to build a facade of a house with a gateway to block out the view, otherwise we would have had nothing on that side of the road of any period – it was all modern.'

Since there were shots of the old house on film from the earlier series, the crew were able to build the facade as an identical match to its predecessor. From the outside, it looks like a perfectly ordinary hardware shop but once visitors try the door and find it doesn't open, they become suspicious. They have then been seen tapping the walls, only to discover that they're made of plywood. Next they go to the genuine courthouse next door and start tapping that in a bid to find the join. Another fake is the post box outside the tea room which plays Ballykissangel post office. So many visitors were posting letters there that the crew had to seal up the box.

Ballykissangel Post Office is really a converted tea room. The genuine post office in Avoca is situated on the other side of the bridge but has not been used for filming.

'There was even talk of building a facade of the whole village in the studio,' continues Paul Harrison, 'because shooting has now become quite difficult in

Avoca. We feel a bit like a sideshow and while we don't want to restrict the public – because you must never do that – some of them have no idea about filming and will rush up to Stephen in the middle of a take. We were in the middle of a really hard shoot last year and it was eighty degrees on the tarmac, the traffic was stretching back in every direction, my assistant director was tearing his hair out because there was too much noise to get the shot done and I said: "Don't look now, but there's sixty blue-haired old ladies racing up the road shouting, "We want the priest! We want the priest!" '

Director Paul Harrison mulls things over with Stephen Tompkinson who plays Father Clifford.

Location manager Luke Johnston acts as the buffer between the film crew and the public. He says: 'I have to let people know about the circus that is about to descend upon them. And we have to be careful that while we get what we need to film, we don't steamroller over other people.

'Practically every property in Avoca has our paint on it. There are often three or four houses in a row owned by the same person and so they're all painted the same colour. Therefore in order to make it look more villagey and to break it up a bit, we paint the houses different colours so that they look like separate properties. Before we do so, we say to the houseowner: "If you like the colour, we'll leave it on; but if at the end of the shoot you don't, we'll have it re-decorated."

'My job is the best excuse to be nosy. When I'm location hunting, if anything looks remotely interesting, I'll go up to the door and talk to the owner. You have to be honest with them and say that it will be a huge disruption to their daily routine, that people will be coming in and moving their furniture around and they'll hardly be able to move. Some will say no, but others might be interested if the price is right. The money householders are paid for location work depends on the length of shooting and the amount of disruption, but our aim is always to leave places the way we find them, or better if we can.

'Madge and Gerald Valentine, who own the house we use as Quigley's, are always delighted to have us. They're on first-name terms with all of the crew and make a point of joining us for breakfast. Last year they let us put up a false door inside the house for Quigley's sauna and a jacuzzi outside. When we weren't filming, they took family photos of themselves in the jacuzzi out on the verandah. They said the children loved it.

'Ireland is very small anyway so you can find practically anything in Ireland somewhere, but County Wicklow in particular has such a range of scenery. You've got the sea, lakes, blasted heaths, mountains, valleys and lush farmland although we avoid showing the sea because we don't want to specify exactly where Ballykissangel is supposed to be.

'Not only have the people of Avoca been magnificent but the Garda have been very amenable and generous with their time. It would have been very difficult to film without their cooperation. Last year, we were on a night shoot in Avoca and it was about ten o'clock when the Gard turned to me and apologised for having to leave us for a while because he had to go and search for a missing person. When we finished at one in the morning, he was still out searching so he would have had a really long night. But even in those circumstances they are always considerate.'

Three weeks before the first block of filming in Avoca, the *Ballykissangel* construction team paint the village to look the same as it did the year before. For production designer David Wilson, this can be a harrowing time. 'Every time we give the villagers more money, they change the place. This year we found that the priest had put new lights into the church. Last year we came down and he was merrily painting the railings and the walls of the church. We said: "But you promised you wouldn't touch the place!" And he said: "But I thought a little tidy-up wouldn't do any harm." Understandably they want to make it tidy for the tourists, especially as St Mary and Patrick's – which we use as St Joseph's – has probably had more in its donation box than ever before in its history.

'Again last year, we found they'd put new tarmac on the car park and were building a big grotto in the corner. There was this huge statue. They said: "Some nuns gave us a statue so we thought we'd build a grotto!" All of these things muck up our continuity, but you can't really stop them.'

The studio set of Fitzgerald's is a fairly faithful reproduction of its real-life counterpart. There is an old map of Wicklow on the wall, together with a bookcase, framed pictures and old Guinness advertisements. The main difference is that in the real Fitzgerald's, most of the pictures on the wall are of the cast and crew of *Ballykissangel*. There is also considerably more space behind the bar in the studio version to allow for cameras. David Wilson says: 'We've recently added a toilet and cellar to the pub set and we've re-designed it so that we can float some of the walls out. Our directors are in there so long that the lack of space was becoming claustrophobic. So now a lot of the walls are on wheels.

'As the Christmas show features a mining accident, we've built our own mine in the studio out of wood and plaster. We built the entrance to the mine near Avoca, at the top of a mountain, and dug down a little way to make it look more authentic. To match it up, I took plaster casts of the rocks there. Avoca used to be a mining village and one of the old copper mines is now the local dump so I must admit I got funny looks for wanting to take rock samples from the dump! I tried to get into the old mines, but it's impossible as they've all been closed off and you can't find the entrances any more. But one of the locals took us up into the mountains where there's an old gold mine which apparently nobody knows about. So I was able to have a look in that as a basis for my studio reconstruction.'

The seventy-five-minute Christmas special plus the eleven episodes in the third series of *Ballykissangel* were filmed over a total of twenty-nine weeks. The task of arranging accommodation for the British cast and crew fell to production coordinator Liza Buckley. 'There are really only half a dozen places to stay in Avoca,' says Liza, 'and we are constantly mindful of not booking up all the best accommodation in the area so that there is none left for the tourists. That simply wouldn't be fair. So we tend to spread out with a lot of people staying nearer Dublin. And we keep our artists well away from Fitzgerald's in case they end up being bought free drinks all night and wake up with a raging hangover!'

Production manager Noëlette Buckley (no relation) is responsible for putting together the crew and generally ensuring that the production is running smoothly. She says: 'The politics of Avoca are very important on the production and we never make any decision without thinking of the people there. For any inconvenience we might cause — and we have had to erect barricades to control the crowds — we like to put something back into the community. For example, we get our caterers to buy all their meat from the butcher in Avoca, rather than elsewhere. It keeps him happy.'

Where *Ballykissangel* is concerned, the world of production buyer Robert Jones seems to revolve around buses and sheep. He reveals: 'Our vehicle coordinator Reggie Blain found Father Clifford's black Jowett Javelin car (which belongs to a family in Northern Ireland) and the famous old Ballykissangel bus. It's simply a question of having the right contacts. Similarly for the third series, Padraig, the garage owner, buys an old burger van. I phoned a caterer and he put me in touch with a guy called

Patsy Gray who had a fleet of half a dozen burger vans. And among them was this amazing 1960s model, pale blue with big chrome sides and decorated with a huge picture of a cowboy. It was beautifully tacky – just right for the job.

'We get our animals from local farmers. Eamonn's pigs were supplied by Phil Wheatley who has also lent us goats and turkeys. The pigs were a bit excitable so we had to bring them in three days before we were ready to film and build a special sty for them. We treat them as we would any actor – maybe better! We get our sheep from Norrie McGee, another local farmer, who is a wonderful shepherd and has hundreds of sheep. Not that many people in Ireland watch TV, especially farmers, so it's all a bit of a novelty to them and they're keen to help.'

But surely Robert's oddest request surrounded Niamh's pregnancy when he was asked to produce a knitted uterus. 'It was for Niamh's ante-natal classes and there is a scene where the midwife demonstrates the birth with this knitted uterus. She pulls back the lip, the head of a baby doll pops out and Ambrose faints. When it first appeared in the script, the producer queried it, the director queried it and I queried it, but the writer was adamant that such a thing existed. But I knew it wasn't something I'd be able to get in a shop so I had to ask Jean, the lady who does all my drapes: "Can you knit me a uterus?" It's a good job I know her! Anyway, she got to work and knitted me a lifelike replica in red chunky wool. And everyone was happy, although to my eyes it looked more like a haggis.'

Father Clifford's black Jowett Javelin car.

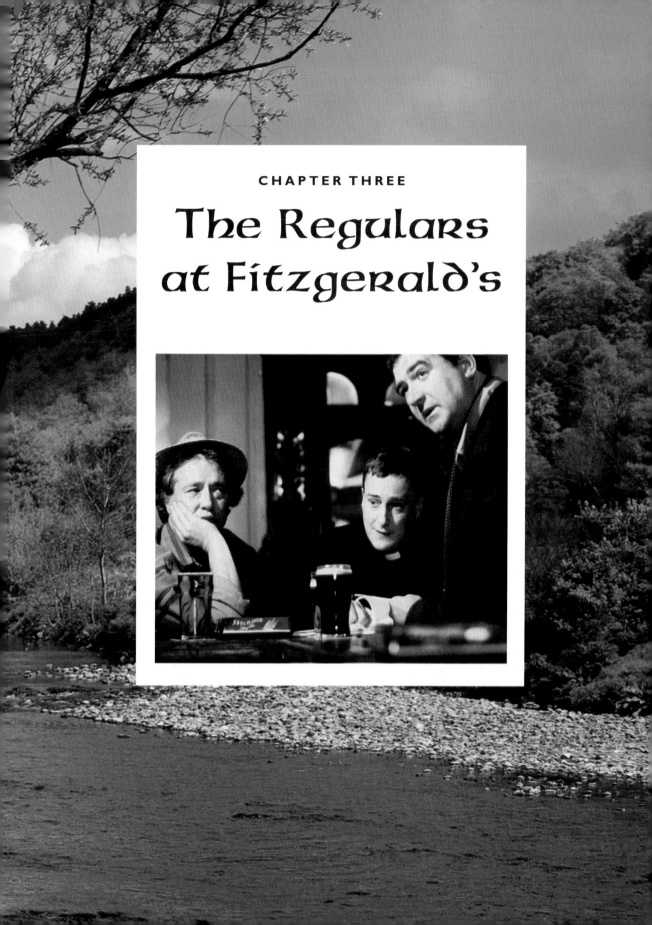

CHAPTER THREE

The Regulars at Fitzgerald's

FATHER PETER CLIFFORD

played by STEPHEN TOMPKINSON

Father Peter Clifford,
the city boy transferred
to the country.

PREVIOUS PAGE *Padraig,*
Father Clifford and
Brendan Kearney prop up
the bar in the studio set
of Fitzgerald's.

If childhood dreams had been fulfilled, Stephen Tompkinson might today have been serving as a priest, instead of playing one. 'I was brought up as a Catholic and went to a Catholic school in Lytham St Annes, Lancashire, and I think that at ten or eleven I quite fancied the idea of becoming a priest. Priests were always there, very much part of your life, in and out of your house, drinking your parents' alcohol. They were part of the family. In that sort of background, you have a leaning towards the priesthood when you are young because it's the most glamorous job you are introduced to. Then along came puberty, sport and girls, and that was the end of that idea!

'Even so I was an altar boy until I was sixteen and I was doing readings until I was eighteen, so I know all the workings of Mass and I still go whenever I can. I've still got my faith. And my own local priest was another Father Mac – Father McIlroy.

'Funnily enough, it was one of the things which never came up in the audition for Father Clifford – are you a Catholic? Maybe there just wasn't time because it all happened in such a hurry. I was sent Kieran Prendiville's script and I thought it was superb, so different from anything else on television at the time. My audition was two o'clock on the Wednesday afternoon. Joy Lale was there, along with director Richard Standeven, and executive producers Tony Garnett and Robert Cooper. I went in, read a couple of scenes and got home where I received a call at five o'clock asking whether I could fly to Dublin that night for a screen test in the morning. I said, "Yes…OK." I flew over on Wednesday night and was given three more scripts, which were fantastic. I was completely hooked. I didn't sleep at all – it was one of those things when you want something so much.

'The screen test was directed by Richard Standeven at ten o'clock. After that, I paced the streets for a while, got to the airport about twelve-thirty, phoned my agent and found out that I'd landed the part. Terrific! I went back home to London and then packed and flew to Belfast on the Friday morning for a live radio show in the evening. I stayed the night in Belfast, flew back to London on the Saturday, packed my bags on the Sunday and flew back to Dublin to start work on *Ballykissangel* on the Monday morning!

'They had cast every member of the village first, because that's the title of the programme, and cast the priest, the outsider, last. I knew Dervla before – we'd done a radio play together – and I knew Tony Doyle through working with his daughter Susannah on *Drop the Dead Donkey,* and I'd also met Peter Caffrey once. But the other members of the cast were just faces and names. So on the first day of rehearsals, I felt in the same situation as Father Clifford. That first morning was terrifying. I kept thinking that all these Irish actors would resent someone coming over and nicking the best part, so I was a bit dry in the mouth.'

To add to Stephen's sense of isolation, apart from the short trip to Dublin for the screen test, this was his first visit to Ireland. 'Although three out of my four grandparents were Irish, my mum's not a great traveller so family holidays used to be confined to England, Scotland or Wales. Ireland was somewhere I was always desperate to go to and *Ballykissangel* turned out to be the perfect excuse. I immediately fell in love with the country and the people. I love filming over here, the pace of life is completely different. It's everything you ever heard about the Irish being warm and hospitable, and more. People have the time of day for you, strangers are prepared to talk to you. And Avoca is superb – it's everything you want it to be in the script.'

Father Clifford and Niamh enjoying the Ballykissangel Festival.

Stephen was born in Lytham St Annes thirty-one years ago. His father worked in a bank and his mother was a teacher. 'We get on just great as a family,' says Stephen, 'nauseatingly well, very strong and close-knit. My father and his elder brother married my mother and her elder sister, so you are extra close when two brothers are married to two sisters. All my grandparents have gone now, sadly, but one grandfather was a huge influence on me. He was very like Stan Laurel, a real, natural, gentle comic. I found him adorable.'

Stephen's acting ambitions were encouraged at school. 'There were proper facilities, a stage and lights and teachers who were prepared to give up their spare time to put on plays. They encouraged the children to use their imagination, to let it run wild. I owe them a lot.'

Since leaving drama school, Stephen has spent just three weeks out of work and that was by choice because he wanted to see a Test match in Australia. 'I love cricket and play whenever I can. In fact, I'm mad about most sports,' adds the self-confessed Middlesbrough fan (his family live in Stockton-on-Tees).

He first made his mark in 1990 as Globelink's ruthless newshound Damien Day in *Drop the Dead Donkey*, a role for which he was voted best comedy actor at the 1994 British Comedy Awards. 'Damien and Father Clifford are diametrically opposed roles. They're like twins separated at birth – one became a journalist, the other a priest! I'm somewhere in between the two of them, trying to stay sane.'

He went on to play DC Park in *Minder*, Spock in *All Quiet on the Preston Front*, Mark in the sitcom *Downwardly Mobile* with Josie Lawrence, and Jeremy Craig in the Screen Two production *A Very Open Prison*. Last year he made his movie debut in *Brassed Off*, alongside Pete Postlethwaite, Tara Fitzgerald and Ewan McGregor. But it is the role of Father Peter Clifford that has really captured the public's imagination.

The second son of five children to an Irish GP (now deceased) who had settled in a North of England mill town, Peter Clifford was brighter than average for his age. He attended the local grammar school where he preferred science to the arts and football to cricket. From there, he progressed to university where he studied astronomy and then, to his mother's delight, he discovered that he had a vocation to the priesthood. So he joined the seminary at Allen Hall in London before being posted to an inner-city parish in Manchester where he proved himself to be decent, hardworking and compassionate. He held fairly liberal views which meant that he was inclined to let individual conscience hold sway over religious dogma.

His problem was that he was becoming a bit cocky. He began to enjoy his standing in the community, the respect, the reverence and the love – a little too much love in the case of Jenny, a single mother. Jenny confessed her feelings for him and, despite his best efforts and the fact that nothing actually happened between them, Peter could feel himself falling in love with her. Faced with a straight choice – Jenny or the job – he asked for a transfer. His bishop decided to try and put as much distance between Peter and Manchester as he could, so he phoned a colleague in Ireland and arranged for Peter to be posted to County Wicklow. Thus he arrived in Ballykissangel, only to be confronted with a new temptation…Assumpta Fitzgerald.

'There's nothing black and white about Peter apart from the clothes he wears,' says Stephen. 'He has a more modern way of thinking which doesn't always go down well with old-fashioned priests. Kieran Prendiville never wrote Father Mac as the baddie – he's just very much a priest of his time. So the two will always clash on certain issues. Father Mac jerks his chain in one direction and Peter is determined to go another way. One of the things people seem to like about Peter is that he doesn't pretend to have all the answers. He never has an ideal solution, but hopefully he can offer a few more options than the Church's traditional point of view.

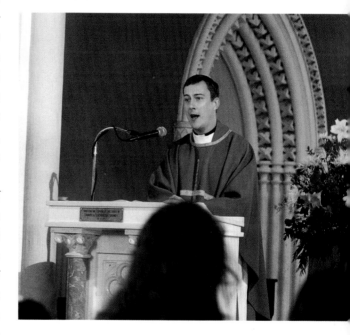

'Peter's self-confidence suffered as a result of the business with Jenny and it took a while to return. He needs to stay where he feels wanted and I think he has made a difference to Ballykissangel. He's certainly not the fish out of water that he was at the start and is much more a member of the community now. He still gets wrong-footed by various people but he's not as green as he was. He's stronger all round and more determined when problems arise. He's also more confident in his dealings with Father Mac, more willing to fight his corner.

Father Clifford's folk Mass, at which Irish rock star Enda Sullivan played guitar, proved an enormous success.

'The show isn't a thing of an Englishman in Ireland, it's more about a city boy being in the country. BallyK is a country environment, with everything that involves. Very often things are not quite what they seem on the surface.'

Right from the start, viewers were intrigued by the relationship between Father Clifford and Assumpta, wondering whether it would ever lead to a full-blooded romance. 'He's quite a good match for Assumpta, who's equally determined, so they get along well, even though originally she didn't like men, priests or the English! But it's not a will-they-won't-they situation. Their relationship is more a marriage of minds. I just think if they ever get it together, the show is over.'

To the delight of the world's press, Stephen and Dervla Kirwan, who plays Assumpta, have got it together. The story of the 'priest' and the 'bar owner' falling in love has proved irresistible to the tabloids whose subsequent antics could have come straight from the Damien Day book of journalism. Stephen reflects: 'They've done things like follow my ex-wife to the shops and camp out on her doorstep, only for her to reveal the shock horror story that we're still great friends and that she's met Dervla. Things have been blown out of proportion by the amount of coverage we've had, but I suppose that's to be expected because the ratings for *Ballykissangel* have been so high.

'But it hasn't changed the chemistry between Peter and Assumpta at all. Dervla is as steeped in her character as I am in mine and, hopefully, we're both good enough actors not to let it interfere. As far as we're concerned, the work and "us" are two entirely different things, and the "us" is very much put on the backburner while we're working.'

Stephen agrees that the 'intriguing forbidden romance' between Father Clifford and Assumpta is part of the appeal of the show. 'But there are also many other reasons for the success of *Ballykissangel*. There's a tremendous sense of community in the show which maybe people don't experience in their own lives. One paper said we had the best acting ensemble ever put together on TV. Who are we to argue? And there's plenty of good drama to balance the lighter side, which makes it perfect Sunday night viewing. It's a nice change from all those hospital and police series. Plus there's the fact that it goes out in February and you see these beautiful postcard pictures of County Wicklow, courtesy of the BBC. If you add all these things together you may go some way to answering why the show has had such public and critical acclaim. Whatever the reasons, I'm absolutely delighted by the response we've had.'

Stephen has had a couple of uncomfortable moments on the series. 'For the scene where I was running through the night to wake Padraig up to get some form of transport to attend a dying man, I must have lost about two inches in height running up the main street in Avoca. It's quite a steep street and we did it well over twenty times. They clocked me at twenty-two miles an hour at one point in the camera truck. And it was all for two seconds of filming!

'Then there was the Gaelic football match where we had players from two local teams with me in goal. I was black and blue after that. Director Richard Standeven had told the lads to really go for it and not pull any punches so they really enjoyed kicking the crap out of a minor celebrity. They were saying to me afterwards: "Yeah, that's my bruise there." "And that one's mine." "And that's mine…"'

ASSUMPTA FITZGERALD

played by DERVLA KIRWAN

Dervla Kirwan is still coming to terms with the incredible public reaction to *Ballykissangel*. 'We were out filming in the summer and a man came over to me, shook my hand and said: "Assumpta, can I touch you?" He wasn't strange or anything, but the moment was almost unreal.

'Generally speaking, people don't quite know how to handle me. They never say anything out of order, which is really nice, and I think it's because Assumpta is quite a fierce character. But it still amazes me that people will travel all this way to Avoca just to see a fictional village.'

Dervla comes from a stable, close-knit, middle-class Dublin family. Her mother taught Latin and French and her father worked in insurance. 'I'm the youngest of three sisters. One sister is an auctioneer and the other's a biochemist. I'm very much the odd one out! We used to have a house in the country about thirty or forty miles from Avoca so I often passed through it.

The beautiful and feisty Assumpta Fitzgerald.

'I was educated at a convent school just outside Dublin but I used to be very shy as a child. Then I started going to drama classes because the other kids in my street were going and I thought it would be fun.'

At the age of fifteen, she was chosen by director Charles Sturridge for the television drama *Troubles,* about life in Northern Ireland. She went on to combine school and theatre work before moving to London at eighteen. Shortly afterwards, she landed the role of a teenage girl with a middle-aged lover in Melvyn Bragg's controversial TV drama *A Time to Dance,* then she signed up to play Phoebe in the BBC comedy *Goodnight Sweetheart*. At the height of the series' success, Dervla decided to leave because she wanted to pursue different roles. And by then she had thrown herself into the part of Assumpta.

'Phoebe and Assumpta couldn't be more different people,' says Dervla. 'It was just coincidence that they both happened to be landladies. Phoebe was very good to me but actually it was nice to get out of those 1940s corsets and clothes. They could be a bit restricting!

'I'd been wanting a part like Assumpta for a long time. Before *Ballykissangel* came along, I'd taken three months off to have a rest and wait for something special. As soon as I read the first script, I knew that this was it. I think in every episode there is a backbone that is quite stark and delivers a message. That's what attracted me immediately when I read it. It's light drama but at the same time I don't think it patronises any Irish person, or English person, which is very important. There's none of that diddly-dee clichéd Irish stuff, thank goodness, but properly drawn, real people.

'It was also great to be back working in Ireland. There's only so much you can take in a big city like London so when the opportunity came to work in Ireland on a good part and a wonderful script, I jumped at it. I knew it would be a great learning process for me, to work with wonderful actors and a brilliant crew.

'I really had to fight for the part, though. I did lots of interviews and about half a dozen screen tests with people who were up for the Father Clifford part. At one point I thought maybe the producers were just using me to test these other guys – you get so bogged down in the auditioning process. I thought: "Am I in with a chance?" But obviously they were looking for two people with the right chemistry. Happily they decided that was Stephen and me.'

After gaining a degree at Dublin University, the beautiful Assumpta inherited Fitzgerald's from her late mother. Then it was an old-style Irish country pub but Assumpta transformed the place into a bar/café where people could go for a meal or a cup of coffee, as well as alcohol. Under her ownership, Fitzgerald's has become the social hub of Ballykissangel.

Assumpta's dislike of the clergy dates back to childhood. Her parents separated when she was young, but not before priests had tried to force them to stay together, an action which brought misery to the entire family. So she despises everything Father Mac stands for. Indeed, she barely tolerates him. She would like Peter more if he wasn't a priest, but finds it hard to separate the man from the dog collar. She doesn't make a great living out of Fitzgerald's, and from time to time yearns to return to Dublin. But she has a good relationship with her regulars. Niamh is her best friend, she is very fond of Siobhan and while she disapproves of Quigley's business methods, she respects him…in the way you'd respect a viper.

'Assumpta is a great character for me to play because up to now I've played quite vulnerable parts. Assumpta, on the other hand, is very forthright and opinionated. She speaks her mind, which is refreshing. She certainly doesn't suffer fools gladly and while she is angry, it's not in a nasty way. She's very sardonic, very complex and very deep, and you could confuse tenacity for stubbornness because she has equal amounts of both.

'She was very suspicious of Father Clifford to start with, because of who he is and what he stands for. She also hated the old priest and thought everyone was like him. It's only as she got to know the new man that she realised he really cares about people and she grows to like him. In many ways the two of them are kindred spirits, yet they are completely different too. She has met her match in him but is caught off balance in coming across someone who has such a strong faith, while she has none. Both are stubborn and strong-willed and what draws her to him is that he doesn't back down, even in the face of real opposition.

'It's lucky really because the way *Ballykissangel* is written needs the sexual chemistry between Assumpta and Peter to work, and the relationship between Stephen and me just gives it an extra charge.

'The part was brilliantly written by Kieran Prendiville and any actress would have had to be blind not to hit the mark the way he led,' adds Dervla modestly. That there was more to it than that was reflected by the fact that she was voted Most Popular Actress in the 1996 National Television Awards.

Like Assumpta, Dervla is no longer a practising Catholic. 'I find the whole idea of the old-fashioned Catholic religion rather off-putting and oppressive. I think the beliefs need modernising and bringing up to date.' But she is understandably keen to point out that she and Assumpta are two entirely different people. 'She's not me. When you play a part in your own accent, perhaps you have less to hide behind and you bring in more of your own

Assumpta occasionally gets itchy feet to return to Dublin.

experiences, but you're still not that person. Sure, I have an affinity with her and I like lots of things about her, although maybe she should try and channel her anger in a different way. She could try kick-boxing or lots of evening primrose oil… In fact, I've modelled parts of her on people I grew up with at school.

'I got the part when I was twenty-three (I'm twenty-five now) and I think it adds to the mystique as to how someone that young survives running a bar. I talked to friends who own a pub in Dublin because I had to understand the business of running a bar, which is quite tricky, and find out how dedicated she'd have to be to make it work. And I did a lot of research sitting in Dublin bars, just to get that right-arm action. Very important!'

However, the third series of *Ballykissangel* will be Dervla's last. 'The decision to leave has been tortuous,' she admits, 'and I'm sure I'll get a lot of flak in the press about it. But it's the same with any job – it's important to move on from time to time. I get itchy feet and I feel that now is the right time for me to move on.'

BRIAN QUIGLEY

played by TONY DOYLE

Businessman Brian Quigley,
the chancer of BallyK.

OPPOSITE *While Quigley*
conducts the bidding, Donal
parades Assumpta as one of
the lots at the Ballykissangel
Slave Auction. The unlikely
figure of Father Mac finally
secured her services.

Trying to get a straight answer out of Tony Doyle is like trying to conduct a straight deal with Brian Quigley. Tony has a wisecrack for every question. Ask him whether there is any part of him in Quigley and he'll pat his backside and say, 'Yes, this part.' Ask him the secret of the show's success and he will reply with a perfectly straight face, 'Me.'

But with perseverance the affable Tony will open up and reveal his thoughts on the business brain that is Brian Quigley. The proprietor of Quigley Developments, Quigley is the 'Mr Big' of Ballykissangel, a man with an insatiable desire to make money, regardless of whether it is strictly legal. A successful builder and active member of the Community Council and Chamber of Commerce, he likes to think he runs the town and has major plans for turning it into a tourist centre. To this end, he has set about acquiring as much property in the area as he can with a view to creating holiday homes. He has lived in BallyK most of his life, apart from doing a business studies course in Dublin and enjoying a profitable period in the UK where he made sufficient money to launch his empire back in Ireland. Widowed in 1990, he is very close to his daughter Niamh. Although not religiously inclined, he likes to maintain links with the Church, realising that it still has power and influence, and so keeps in with the equally manipulative Father Mac.

'Quigley is definitely a member of the family of loveable rogues,' says Tony. 'He knows no fear. If he sees the potential in some deal or other to make money, he goes for it and doesn't count the cost until it's all over. Business is business! He barges in where others might think twice, and he's done well for himself out of it. True, some of his more spectacular schemes have flopped, but at least they've been spectacular flops!

'But the thing about *Ballykissangel* is that it's not all warmth and humour. It has the odd trauma and tragedy too. It doesn't avoid the more serious issues that hit you in the face from time to time, and most episodes chew over one serious subject or another. This hard edge gives a richness to the stories and to the

characters because they don't just fulfil one function of buffoon or whatever. All the characters are three-dimensional, weighty and fulsome. Quigley is more than a comic character. He may be up to some devilish roguery but he's also got a very good relationship with his daughter, so you see the man behind the mask.

'He and Niamh might not always appear to be close because they're quite tough with each other, but there's a very strong bond between them. It's the kind of blood tie which displays itself at difficult times, often tragic times, when families come together for each other. And Quigley likes the fact that Niamh stands up to him. He's pleased that she's the person she is because it means she's more than capable of looking after herself.

'He also has a good relationship with Father Mac. They understand each other and although they try and use each other, they don't fall out over anything. Father Mac can invariably outmanoeuvre Quigley. Quigley is more the general in the field while Father Mac is the War Office!

'Quigley might think he can manipulate Ambrose, but he can't. The position of the policeman in the Irish community is quite unique – they're very highly regarded and get on extremely well with the locals. So although Ambrose sticks rigidly to the letter of the law, he is still respected. And I think that's one of the key points about the characters – despite

For once Quigley gets his hands dirty as his slave duties involve unblocking Liam's drains.

occasional conflicts of interest, everybody in BallyK respects everyone else.

'It seems that people are somehow bewitched and enchanted by the idea of this mythical village and these wonderful characters. It's sheer magic, I think, but still indefinable. My twelve-year-old son says he likes *Ballykissangel* because it "makes you feel warm". I know it's well written and well acted and they say it has a certain charm, but charm doesn't often sell television drama — grit and angst usually do that. But it seems to make people feel good and if the British people want to experience it first hand, then they are only fifty minutes away. *Ballykissangel* is certainly great publicity for Ireland, instead of the negative side, and it is actually a truer reflection of Irish life.'

The youngest of four children, Tony was born in County Roscommon in the West of Ireland. He went to boarding school in Dublin when he was twelve and his family later relocated to the capital, but he remains a country boy at heart.

'To an extent, *Ballykissangel* has resonances for me of my own upbringing. I had a good time as a child, but we didn't have all the trappings of modernity that people have today. Most people got around on bicycles. There was certainly nothing like Quigley's Land Rover in the vicinity, that's for sure.'

Tony moved to London in the 1960s and in recent years home for him, his second wife Sally and their three children has been in Brittany, with school holidays spent in London. But he has been in such demand of late that the principal family home has now switched back to London. For Tony Doyle is one of our most underrated actors, able to convey an air of subtle menace beneath a respectable veneer. His TV credits include *Children of the North, Perfect Scoundrels, Taggart, Peak Practice, Band of Gold, Castles* and *Between the Lines* in which he was outstanding as bent copper John Deakin. Both Joy Lale and Richard Standeven worked with him on *Between the Lines*.

Tony has been described as Ireland's answer to Jack Nicholson. 'Others obviously see me very differently from how I see myself. People seem to see the dark side in me, or the dark side of themselves in me. I don't know which. Quigley's certainly an enigma, though he cracks a few jokes like some of the other characters I've played. He definitely has his lighter side.'

Although the majority of his work has been in England, Tony always enjoys returning to Ireland. 'There's just a very special atmosphere here, which is caring and embracing but also gives you space to actually do the work. There isn't that sense of colossal pressure that you might get working in a city such as London though up until fairly recently, Ireland didn't really get the benefit of major investment in film and television.

'Of course *Ballykissangel* is a big project, but because it's filmed here, there is still that special atmosphere which eases the pain of all the fourteen- or fifteen-hour days. The work gets done but everybody still enjoys each other's company. We're a bit like a very large, extended family and hopefully a lot of that special atmosphere translates itself onto the screen.'

NIAMH QUIGLEY

played by TINA KELLEGHER

Quigley's strong-willed daughter Niamh.

'I'm pregnant again,' laughs Tina Kellegher. The actress best known for her portrayal of single mum Sharon in the BBC film version of Roddy Doyle's *The Snapper* (a role for which she won the Best Newcomer award at the Geneva Film Festival) is with child once more, this time as Brian Quigley's strong-willed daughter Niamh.

'I seem to specialise in playing pregnant women,' says Tina. 'I don't know why — maybe I look a bit "mumsy". The first time I had to be pregnant, I got books from the library, talked to friends and generally made myself a walking expert on giving birth. Now I'm a bit of an old hand.'

Recently married to Ambrose, Niamh is Quigley's only daughter. Although she loves her father, she is not blind to his faults and sometimes finds herself experiencing a conflict of loyalties when he is on one side of the law and her husband is on the other. She has experienced more than her share of heartache, first losing her mother and then suffering a miscarriage. Now she is praying for better luck with her second pregnancy. She is great friends with Assumpta and from time to time indulges in bouts of matchmaking in an attempt to provide Assumpta with the same sort of idyllic relationship which she enjoys with Ambrose.

'Niamh is a bit of a Jewish princess,' says Tina. 'She is the centre of her father's life and he has spoilt her something rotten. She's very like her father. She shares his determination and I suppose they're both bullies — they see things their own way and like to get their own way. I think he likes to see himself in her...unless of course she's giving him a lot of stick about something. For while she'll help him if she can as long as what he's up to is legal, she gives him a wide berth when he's doing something dodgy. But although they have their clashes, they love each other to death.

'One of the things which attracted me to the part was the fact that Niamh had lots of colour and possibilities because although she can be forceful, she's also got a big heart. I think she's mellowed since marriage and is more self-assured. She takes her status in the community very seriously — it was very important for her to acquire the position of married woman. But she can still blow hot air and get nowhere fast since nobody takes her seriously other than herself, which is fun to play.

'She and Ambrose are a lot closer since the miscarriage. At first she tried to control him but he's proved himself to her. Besides, I think she likes it when he stands up to her – in fact, it's a real turn-on for her. She was very methodical about getting pregnant in the first place and approached it with almost military precision, calling him home when the time was right to do the job. A friend of mine told me that he was round at the house of a friend who was trying for a baby, and while they were chatting, the wife called her husband upstairs to do his duty. Apparently it was like training for a marathon!'

The daughter of a garage manager, Tina grew up in Cavan as one of six children. 'From about the age of ten I did stand-up comedy and impersonations – people like Margaret Thatcher, Shirley Bassey and Lena Zavaroni. I just found I had a gift for mimicry. Then I started solo singing but from the moment I did my first straight play, I realised that I wanted to act, rather than sing or tell jokes, and I went on to serve my apprenticeship at the Druid Theatre, Galway. Apart from an uncle who was an actor in Belfast, I was the first member of my family to go into drama. However, my mother is a great singer and would like to have been a professional, so she's delighted about what I've achieved so far. So is my father, now he knows I can earn a living. He was very anxious about the insecurity of the profession, but as soon as I started getting a wage at the Druid, he was happy enough.'

Niamh confronts husband Ambrose getting out of the bath. A misplaced bar of soap was to lead to his downfall.

Much of Tina's work has been in the theatre although she did appear on TV in *Murder in Eden* (which also featured Tony Doyle) and *The Hanging Gale* as well as in films such as *Widow's Peak* and *In the Name of the Father*. She admits to being unsure about the prospect of becoming a familiar face in people's living rooms. 'I find that a bit frightening. I didn't go into the business to be a celebrity. I just wanted to work and to be challenged by roles.'

And she confesses to initial doubts as to how *Ballykissangel* would be received by the Irish public. 'But it hasn't been a problem. People in Ireland thought that various issues might be clichéd but *Ballykissangel* deals with things in a fresh and honest way. I think we've taken the clichéd images and set-ups and stood them on their heads. To my mind, part of the reason the show works is its undoubted feelgood factor. There's no stress to it and that's what people want on a Sunday evening before setting off for a hard week's work.'

The series has also provided Tina with a welcome break from some of her more harrowing roles. 'I have done a lot of angst-ridden victimised women, so it's refreshing to play somebody who is a bit of fun…even though she is pregnant.'

Niamh urges Ambrose to turn a blind eye when the villagers decide to stage a poker tournament at Fitzgerald's.

AMBROSE EGAN

played by PETER HANLY

Peter Hanly admits that he gets some puzzled looks from passers-by when he's out on the streets filming as Gard Ambrose Egan, Ballykissangel's law enforcement officer. 'Often when we're filming in Avoca, there are long tailbacks of cars,' says thirty-two-year-old Peter, 'and people see me standing in the middle of the road in my uniform and wonder why I'm not helping to sort out the traffic jams. Then after a while they spot the cameras and realise I'm an imposter.'

Peter says he didn't do a great deal of research for the role of Ambrose. 'Basically, I've just chatted to the Gards in Avoca and Enniskerry. Ironically, one of the Gards in Enniskerry is called Pat Ambrose! I've never got a fully honest opinion from the Gards as to what they think of my portrayal, nor have I looked for one, although they did suggest that I perfect my salute. Generally we just joke in passing and they make

Gard Ambrose Egan, an uncompromising law enforcer.

comments like "officious and helpful as usual". But I think they probably approve of Ambrose because he is conscientious and honest and actually very good at his job.'

Deeply religious, open-faced, intelligent and dedicated to upholding the law to the point of being a zealot, Ambrose is a key figure in the local community. His only vice is being a fan of the Nolans.

'People have described him as gormless and naïve,' says Peter, 'and sometimes he is, but I've never wanted him to be a real "eejit". It's really the fact that he's so officious which makes him look silly. The first impressions of Ambrose are that he's old-fashioned for his age and very conservative – he didn't want to live or sleep with Niamh before they were married. He takes his job very seriously so he can be a bit prim and po-faced on occasions, which is why he deserves to have the mickey taken out of him to some extent. In fact, it's more than a job to him – it's a vocation. He sticks rigidly to the letter of the law and will dish out parking tickets to anyone, even friends like Assumpta. He tends to think that the right way of doing something is the *only* way.

A crestfallen Ambrose
recovering from his injury.

'Even though his father-in-law, Quigley, writes Ambrose off as ineffectual and foolish, Ambrose doesn't let him get away with anything. Quigley certainly hasn't got him in his pocket. And although at first Niamh was definitely the one who wore the trousers, Ambrose has proved that he can be just as stubborn as her. I'm aware that *Ballykissangel* is mainly for an English audience so I don't want to play an Irish policeman as too much of a fool. Besides, Niamh's no fool and I don't think she'd have married one. She wouldn't want someone she could walk all over. Indeed, it's a foolish criminal who underestimates Ambrose Egan.'

Peter believes the character has plenty of untapped potential. 'The world which Ambrose polices is very gentle. There's no inner-city drugs or anything like that, although he did deal with the case of the wife-beater and there is a little more serious police work in the third series. I think he is ambitious, but when there was the prospect of him being posted to Dublin, he made it clear that he didn't want to go. And that was for family reasons – he likes living in BallyK. But I think it would be great fun if he were drafted in to do undercover work in the neighbouring town of Cilldargan, to see how he would cope in a bigger environment.'

The youngest of three children of a Dublin teacher, Peter was inspired to act at the age of thirteen after seeing his brother performing in a school production of *Henry V*. 'I went on to do school plays but when I left school, I didn't really know what I wanted to do. I had this notion of wanting to become an actor but I didn't know how to go about it. Over the next two years I wandered from one temporary clerical position to another but I was really just waiting to build up the courage to try and get into acting. Meanwhile I had joined the Dublin Youth Theatre, and that gave me the confidence as well as the professional contacts. In the end I thought, "If I don't try acting, I'll regret it for ever."'

Peter has gone on to establish himself as one of Ireland's leading young actors in a string of stage productions including *The Gay Detective* in which he played a gay sergeant in the Dublin police force. 'It was something of a contrast to playing Ambrose,' reflects Peter. He was also chosen by none other than Mel Gibson to play Prince Edward in the Oscar-winning *Braveheart*. 'I was offered it after meeting Mel Gibson and a roomful of associate producers and casting people. Mel didn't ask anyone to audition by reading from a script – he just wanted to meet and have a chat. It was all very exciting.

'And when I read the script for *Ballykissangel*, I thought, "I can do this. It will be fun." I never imagined it would be so successful, but it just seems to have touched a chord, and even some of my most cynical friends have told me they enjoy it. And it's nice to get letters from the public about Ambrose. One asked: "Is there a Peter Hanly fan club?" I had to reply: "Sadly, not yet." But I live in hope…'

FATHER FRANK MACANALLY

played by NIALL TOIBIN

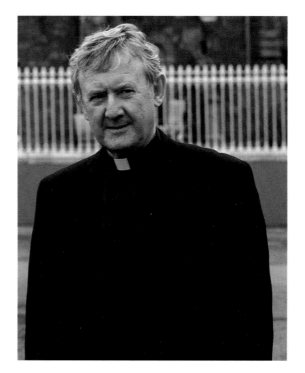

Niall Toibin was on holiday in Israel when he was invited by the Irish delegation to the United Nations to have lunch in the UN canteen. 'I'd just sat down when who should walk in but Yasser Arafat's nanny with Yasser Arafat's baby in a baby walker. The nanny looked straight across at me and exclaimed: "My God, it's Father Mac!" It turns out that she's an English girl whose mum lives in Galway. As she asked me for my autograph, I said to her: "This is about as zany a situation as you could get…"'

As one of the best-known faces on Irish television, Niall is used to being recognised wherever he goes. 'Recently I was at Mass in my own local church and it was a bit long. As I was coming out, one of the priests said to me: "I didn't realise you were here – you could have come in and given us a hand." And I said: "Yes. I could have cut it shorter!" I think he felt the same because the chap who was conducting it was a visiting priest.

Father Mac is short for MacAnally but it could just as easily be Machiavelli.

'I've based Father Mac on an amalgam of many priests and senior Christian brothers that I remember from my schooldays. I didn't need to talk to any priests specifically for this role because I know so many anyway. None of the clergy has taken offence at Father Mac, although when I met my own parish priest in the street, he told me: "You're doing a great job as Father Mac, but I'm afraid the days are long gone when you could treat your curate like that." His voice was tinged with regret…

'There are very few of Father Mac's breed left now. He's typical of an Irish parish priest of about thirty years ago, but there are still a handful of his age around who haven't changed their ways. He's a survivor from an earlier era when the power of the parish priest was unquestioned and still subscribes to the views of the early 1960s.

'He's a very intelligent man and also a realist and I think he genuinely resented the arrival of Father Clifford, not because he was English, but because he represents a liberality in the Church which Father Mac regards as heresy. Father

Mac is a conservative and a traditionalist and he doesn't like having this "liberation theologian", as he calls Father Clifford, under his feet. Even so, he is a man of the people because he does understand local problems. He's not averse to going in the pub and likes to keep in touch with what's going on. He's got a shrewd idea of what everybody's getting up to.

'He's a schemer and as much of a politician as any of the elected ones, which makes him much more interesting to play. But he does have his own integrity and would always be able to justify his political manoeuvrings. He wouldn't regard himself as a schemer – more of a diplomat. He has a certain contempt for almost everyone around him and uses his acerbic tongue to cut people down with sarcasm. He is also offended by vulgarity in speech – in the grammatical sense. He hates wrong usage of words! But at the same time he is prepared to overlook any lack of learning in the likes of Quigley.

'Father Mac is a lot brighter than Quigley – indeed, he's the sharpest person in the parish. He has no illusions about Quigley, and his relationship with him is the result of an absolutely pragmatic decision on Father Mac's part to align himself with Quigley on the basis that the parish will need money now and again. Then he can always put the squeeze on Quigley in a purely commercial way. He manipulates Quigley and is quite prepared to use him then, if necessary, drop him in it. The pair of them have mutually beneficial arrangements but in the end it's always likely to be Quigley who's hung out to dry if things go wrong, while Father Mac walks away. He is extremely adept at distancing himself from the action at the first sign of trouble.

'Indeed, for a man of his obvious abilities and intellect, it is a bit of a mystery as to why he is buried away in a country parish.'

When Niall was growing up in Cork City, entering the priesthood was a popular career choice for many young Irishmen but he was never tempted to become a man of the cloth. 'When I was a kid, every mother hoped that one of her family would become a priest, but mine never mentioned it to me.'

Instead, inspired by listening to Tommy Handley's *ITMA* shows on the radio, he decided that he wanted to be a performer and began his acting career in 1953 with RTE's Radio Repertory Theatre. He joined the company of the Abbey Theatre, Dublin, in 1967 and has since appeared on stage in New York, London and Dublin in productions such as *Fearless Frank*, *The Iceman Cometh* and *The Borstal Boy*. His numerous TV credits include *The Irish RM*, *Boon*, *Casualty* and *Stay Lucky*.

'I'm no stranger to playing priests. In *Brideshead Revisited*, I played the priest who gave the last rites to Olivier's Lord Marchmain and I was also a priest who ran a youth club in the film about the boxer *Benny Lynch*.

'It was casting director Nuala Moiselle who put me forward for *Ballykissangel*. I was asked to read for both Father Mac and Quigley, which is funny because for years Tony Doyle played a priest in *The Riordans*. Perhaps he said he'd had enough of playing priests!

'I have been completely floored by the show's success. I thought it would maybe get a nice comfortable audience of seven or eight million but I couldn't believe it when the ratings hit fifteen million after three episodes. I think one of the things people like about it is that it's very representative of the general mood towards religion in Ireland today. The attitudes of Assumpta are much more the norm these days than the old-fashioned ones of Father Mac. He has the respect of his parishioners but, with the exception of Kathleen, he wouldn't necessarily have their sympathies for his views. In fact, the show is a fair reflection of Ireland in general because there's a lot of humour and concealment in Irish life.'

Niall has discovered that *Ballykissangel* fans are eager to sing their praises of the show, even in the most unlikely places. 'I was at a wedding in London last year and I was just coming out of the Hyde Park Hotel in my tails. A taxi driver looked at me and said: "Are you getting married, Father, or are you performing the ceremony?" He then proceeded to tell me in great detail what he thought of the show and he knew every single storyline twist of every episode.'

With his traditionalist views, Father Mac resented the arrival of Father Clifford, whom he calls the 'liberation theologian'.

BRENDAN KEARNEY

played by GARY WHELAN

Village schoolteacher Brendan Kearney leads an idyllic life.

For Gary Whelan, playing schoolteacher Brendan Kearney is about as good as life gets. 'I have quite a few things in common with Brendan, not least the fact that we both drink Guinness. This makes life considerably easier when we're filming on the studio set of Fitzgerald's. All the drink there is real because it's very difficult to produce an authentic-looking fake pint of Guinness, and they keep us topped up. We can drink as much as we want while we're filming, although it's not advisable to do so. But of course we don't always take advice! So sometimes we have a few drinks, but only if it suits what's happening in the scene. There are times when you will see Brendan inebriated and I may have decided that the scene could survive with a slight degree of inebriation on my part to give it a kick. But obviously there are limits. You can't go falling around drunk or you'd be sacked. But it makes for a pleasant working environment…

'It's a nice job because Brendan doesn't really have to do anything but be himself. Whatever he's feeling shows in his behaviour, and I really enjoy that as an actor.

'Brendan is a man of habits, the eternal bachelor who likes being single. He stands for freedom and I think he's how most married men would want to be. He says what he wants, he has a well-paid job with a pension, he goes fishing and racing and spends a lot of time in the pub. And when he goes fishing, he'll always have a bottle of wine with him, a nice clean glass and the finest cheese. He is an educated man who dresses very smartly and probably has pretensions of being cleverer than he really is. His accent isn't pure Wicklow – he has an anglicised way about him.

'Providing everything's going his way, Brendan is a happy Paddy,' smiles Gary. 'But if you break his routine – like when the pub ran out of Guinness – he can turn really angry. There was no way he would dream of drinking the beer that made Milwaukee famous or any of that dishwater which passes for lager! He's passionate about things – such as the play which Padraig stole – but also very soft-hearted. The way he talks about orchids and badgers and the things around Ballykissangel show that he is a lover of the environment in which he lives. He sees himself as the civilised face of country life. For instance, when Siobhan asks him to put a stallion to a mare, he finds the idea revolting. In many ways, Brendan *is* Ballykissangel because although he is very much his own man, he still manages to fit in with all the groups.'

In terms of circumstance, Dublin-born Gary is the very opposite of Brendan. He is married to Gabrielle (they grew up in the same street) and is the father of five children, ranging in age from eighteen down to four. 'Nevertheless, within the confines of marriage and having lots of children, I do actually live the same sort of lifestyle as him. For nine months of the year I'm living and working in Dublin as an actor and I have a very free life. So he's very similar to me in many ways.'

After training at RADA, Gary made his fortune in the property business and opened Whelan's pub in Dublin, one of the Irish capital's most popular watering holes. Such has been its success that there is now also a Whelan's in London. 'People say you have a couple of bars but it is Gabrielle who designs and runs them. She is Whelan's. I'm an actor.'

At 6ft 3in tall, Gary has played a number of police roles on television in series such as *Prime Suspect, Brookside, EastEnders* and *The Bill*. 'I did have a run of cop shows but eventually I packed them in because I wanted to explore other characters. I was seen as the archetypal detective inspector, with an air of quiet authority, intelligence and an intimidating stare. As DI Amson in *Prime Suspect*, I cracked the case when John Bowe played the serial killer. In *Brookside*, I was DI Kent who, after investigating the deaths of Sue and Danny Sullivan, pursued Barry Grant with a vengeance for a year and a half. I did have him in jail once and I would have got him in the end but I think *Brookside* decided I was getting so close, they'd better write me out of the series. And in *EastEnders*, I was Detective Sergeant Rich who probed the death of Reg Cox right at the start of the series. I eventually married Debbie Wilkins, played by Shirley Cheriton. In fact I married Shirley twice because I married her in *Angels* too. I still haven't consummated either marriage, I must add!

'Whereas once I was always being offered police roles; now, following the release of the film *Michael Collins*, I'm suddenly being asked to play major gangsters. I played a particularly brutal Dublin detective in the film. He was actually killed in the first fifteen minutes – the first man whom Collins ordered to be shot. A critic told me that he was pleased I had been killed early on because he thought that if I hadn't been killed, I'd have beaten the lot of them. It was a backhanded compliment but I felt rather flattered by it. So now I'm being offered these heavy gangsters, but ones with a high level of intelligence. I suppose it's not that much of a departure from the police roles because there is a knife-edge between being a detective inspector and a thinking criminal. They share many of the same traits, but choose to operate on different sides of the law.'

Gary recalls his audition for *Ballykissangel* with wry amusement. 'I was told that there was a series about to be made called *Ballykissangel* and that there was an interesting character which directors Richard Standeven and Paul Harrison and casting director Nuala Moiselle thought I might be suitable for. Nuala put me forward and as soon as they saw me, I was given the part. I arrived, I read and they said: "Yes, exactly what we think Brendan should be – the eternal bachelor. Are you married?" I said, "I am, with five children." "Oh," they said, "you play against it very well."'

One of Brendan's favourite haunts, with the regulars at Fitzgerald's.

SIOBHAN MEHIGAN

played by DEIRDRE DONNELLY

Siobhan is the local vet. Forty-six and single, she lives alone on the edge of the village and spends her evenings in Fitzgerald's for the craic. She enjoys a flutter on the horses or dogs (for which she appears to receive plenty of inside information) and is a red hot poker player. Men enjoy her company because she is 'one of the boys' and she can usually be found propping up the bar with Padraig and Brendan. Sometimes she drinks too much which can lead to embarrassing situations such as sleeping with Brendan or waking up in a field full of sheep. She has yet to decide which was the more excruciating, but at least the sheep didn't snore.

Kind-hearted vet Siobhan Mehigan.

'I'm very fond of Siobhan,' says Deirdre Donnelly. 'She's simple, uncomplicated and almost child-like. She likes to think she's tough, but she's quite vulnerable underneath. And I believe she's probably a bit lonely – let's face it, her only social outlet is the pub.

'She's got a very generous heart, to the extent that she's fond of Eamonn, who's one of her worst-paying customers. In some respects, she and Eamonn are kindred spirits – they both seem to prefer animals to humans. Just as Eamonn wouldn't dream of slaughtering his pigs for food, Siobhan is definitely soft on her patients. I think she feels more relaxed with animals.'

Deirdre is delighted that Siobhan's work will feature prominently in the third series. 'It's a rural series, so you want to see plenty of animals. Whenever we do animal scenes, we have a real vet on standby, showing you how to hold the animal, what instruments to use. When Siobhan had to deliver a calf, we found a lovely cow that was about to give birth. The vet said that an assistant would hold the tail up while I would stroke and soothe the animal all the time. Fortunately I didn't have to do any scenes with my arm inside the cow – we didn't go as far as *All Creatures Great and Small*.

'The vet also taught me how to take blood samples from a pig and went into great detail as to how you conduct semen tests on a stallion. That was another one I was mightily relieved not to have to do – it could have got a bit tricky!

'The pigs were actually the most bad-tempered animals we've had so far. The sow was particularly angry, and didn't like anyone moving a hand towards her piglets. Once one squealed, the rest started. The owner was on hand and we just had to be patient and wait until the sow calmed down, but she was determined not to make it easy for us. No sooner had we got our camera angles sorted, than she would turn around and we'd have to start again.

'I really enjoy those scenes because it's lovely to get out of the studio. It can get a bit claustrophobic in there, though I suppose a lot of people wouldn't mind being stuck in a "pub" for days on end. It sounds idyllic, being paid to drink, but in fact the scenes in the bar take so long to shoot that it goes pretty flat and doesn't taste very nice. So I tend to keep off it.'

Deirdre, whose sister Terry is an actress in New York, has wanted to act for as long as she can remember. She trained at Dublin's Abbey Theatre and has appeared in series such as *The Irish RM* and *The Riordans*. 'I've done mostly theatre work and *Ballykissangel* is certainly the biggest exposure I've had in England. It's nice when people come up to you in the street and tell you how much they enjoy the series. But I like to return to the theatre whenever I can, if only because it gives me the chance to wear beautiful dresses instead of Siobhan's baggy jumpers and jeans. She really doesn't care about her appearance. She never wears make-up and is usually covered in muck!'

Siobhan and Brendan finished up in a situation both would come to regret.

Deirdre lives by the sea near Dublin with her thirteen-year-old daughter Lucy. 'She has appeared as an extra in a couple of scenes, but I wouldn't encourage her to be an actress yet – I don't want her to lose her childhood. Besides, I think she's much more interested in becoming a writer.

'Being in a long-running series like *Ballykissangel* has meant I've had to turn down a lot of other work, but it's a small price to pay. The show really is a joy to work on. I remember when we did the first series in that hot summer of 1995 and the villagers of Avoca appeared as extras, how amazingly patient they were despite the heat. I'm proud to say that a lot of them have become personal friends.'

PADRAIG O'KELLY

played by PETER CAFFREY

Peter Caffrey is refreshingly honest when discussing why he chose acting as a career. 'I don't come from a theatrical background so I'm very much the black sheep of the family. I'd acted a bit in school plays, but it was at university that I really caught the bug. There was a freshers' week where they try and entice all the new students into joining societies and I went to the various stands, considering my options, until I reached the drama society stand. And on the stand were these three gorgeous girls. When I then found out that the ratio of girls to boys in the drama society was three to one, I was well and truly hooked. That seemed a good enough reason to me to take up acting – much better than talking about art and the cosmos!'

From such unlikely beginnings, Dublin-born Peter has become a familiar face on both sides of the Irish Sea. 'Most of my early work was in Ireland, but about thirteen years ago, I moved to England to star in a production of *Children of a Lesser God* in London's West End. I wanted to spread my wings a bit, so when the chance came to work in London, I jumped at it. And that led to a lot of TV work. You name it, I've done an episode of it – *Boon, Casualty,* even six episodes of *Coronation Street* as Father O'Rourke, Ivy Tilsley's priest. I also appeared in two Carla Lane sitcoms, *Luv* (in which I was Lloyd the chauffeur), and *I Woke Up One Morning* where I was one of a quartet of alcoholics. What with propping up the bar of Fitzgerald's as Padraig, drink has featured fairly heavily in my career!'

'Three years ago I came back to Ireland to do a four-week run on stage… and I'm still here. One job just led to another because there's such a rash of stuff being made here at the moment. There's so much more going on now, compared to when I left. You can't turn a corner without bumping into a film crew or a nineteen-year-old with a brilliant script under his arm. The whole place is really jumping.'

A part of the renaissance has been *Ballykissangel*. 'Apparently Joy Lale had seen me in a play and said, "Get him in." It was my birthday – 18 April – and I said, "You've got to give me a present." So she did – the role of Padraig. He's a

Padraig O'Kelly is a gentle character with hidden depths.

gentle, compassionate character, and we're developing him much more in this series. I feel there are hidden depths to him. There was the play he wrote and the fact that in the bar he will suddenly come up with a word like "schadenfreude". It all hints at a greater learning. Maybe he went to university and ended up running the garage in this small village. While I can prop up the bar with great relish, it will be fascinating to find out more about his background. The BBC like the trio at the bar and there must be some good stories behind these three people in their forties. One of the nice things about *Ballykissangel* is that the production team consult the actors about how they would like to see their characters progress. Deirdre Donnelly, Gary Whelan and myself spent a really rewarding day with executive producer Brenda Reid and script editor Ceri Meyrick, putting forward suggestions. All we know about Padraig is that he lives with his son Kevin, who takes Assumpta's dog Fionn McCool for walks and keeps a pet goat. We've never seen the boy's mother so we don't know whether Padraig is a widower or a divorcee. Padraig could even have buried her in the

Padraig's second home.

garden! I suggested it would be interesting if Kevin's mother proved to be very much alive and came back suddenly with a bolt from the blue for Padraig. But whatever happens, it's nice to be consulted – that doesn't happen on every series.

'The thing about *Ballykissangel* is that although we've dealt with topics such as alcoholism, euthanasia, wife-battering and single motherhood, it's not issue-based. It's very much character-driven. And the public have certainly taken to the characters. I was chased down O'Connell Street by a family from Australia who told me

Garage owner Padraig is a popular member of the local community.

they'd been watching me on TV back home two nights earlier. Apparently the show is huge out there.'

Peter also has high hopes for *I Went Down*, a film set in contemporary Ireland in which he and Tony Doyle play rival gangsters. 'Half the crew from *Ballykissangel* worked on the film and, although it's relatively low budget, it was very well received in Cannes. So we're keeping our fingers crossed.'

A more poignant project for the forty-seven-year-old divorcee is *Even the Taxi Driver Laughed,* a film based on his successful battle against cancer of the floor of the mouth. 'I was diagnosed as having cancer six years ago and was told I had six months to live. Fortunately a new form of radiotherapy was being developed at the time so I gave it a go. The treatment was very intensive and it knocked the socks off me. I wasn't sure whether I'd ever fully regain my speech, and it was nine months before I could really function properly again. I was scared out of my wits but I always had a positive mental attitude, which is vital. You're halfway to winning the battle if you say, "Bugger this, I'm going to beat it!" All the staff at the Royal Marsden Hospital in London where I was treated said it's the kickers, biters and fighters who tend to pull through, and here I am having a great time, drinking pints and chasing young women!

'When I started writing the screenplay for the film, I was determined that it shouldn't be earnest or worthy. It's about how a fella copes when he has landed in the shit. I call it the first sex, rock 'n' roll and cancer movie ever. And there's no way anybody other than me will be playing the lead – I wrote the best part for myself.'

LIAM

played by JOE SAVINO

Liam, always on the lookout for a fast buck.

Whatever he may achieve as an actor, Joe Savino has already earned himself a place as a footnote in rock history as the man who once sacked U2's Adam Clayton from a band.

'I first formed a band in school and went on to play pubs and clubs in Dublin. One of my bands was The Max Quad Band, named after a character on Jethro Tull's "Thick as a Brick" album. We needed a bass player. Adam Clayton was at school with my girlfriend of the time and he had a bass so he joined us. But after a few months I fired him because, although he could play, he had this great ability of either finishing songs before they were over, or else they'd be over and he'd still be playing! That was in about 1977 and he's still a great mate of mine although obviously I don't see him very often these days.'

Born of Italian grandparents, forty-one-year-old Joe has always been an entertainer. While playing in bands, he joined drama school and decided that he wanted to make acting his future career. His big break came in 1984. 'A friend, Paul Mercier, had written this brilliant musical called *Drowning* and he asked me to sing what was to be the single from it. As the main character hadn't been cast, they asked me. I did it and one thing led to another. Since then I've done a lot of theatre work as well as starring in the RTE sitcom *Upwardly Mobile* about a couple who win the lottery and move upmarket, a bit like *The Beverly Hillbillies*. It's now in its third year.

'And I still sing and play with a couple of guys in a Dublin pub on Sunday nights. You know, I'm a much better musician than actor…'

His performance as Quigley's hopeless henchman Liam suggests undue modesty. 'Out of Liam and Donal, Liam is the intelligent one,' laughs Joe, 'but that's not saying much. He just happens to be brighter than Donal. Liam is the eternal optimist. There's an end of the rainbow for him in everything he does, but he never finds it. He always manages to fail at the last hurdle. And if he ever did anything that worked, it would be instant heart attack because he's used to things going wrong so that he can head off in some other direction for another hare-brained scheme, another way of making a fast buck.

'He's brutally enthusiastic. If Quigley said to him, "Liam, go up that mountain, here's a box with a few instructions, set up a rocket launcher", he'd do it. He'd say, "OK, Mr Quigley, do you want it for tomorrow or tonight?" In fact, if Quigley wanted Liam to launch himself, he would…as long as there was a couple of bob in it.

'I've met lots of Liams. Ireland is full of Quigleys with Liams working for them, although they may not be quite as daft as Liam.'

Joe had never worked with Frankie McCafferty, who plays Donal, before *Ballykissangel*. 'I knew him to say hello to as a fellow actor, but our paths hadn't really crossed. We soon hit it off, however, and the chemistry between us has built up with the looks we give each other and the way we say things. About halfway through the first series I began to think of us as a double act. Now we're nearly always treated as a pair – we can't function individually!'

Liam's trademark yellow baseball cap was the brainchild of costume designer Maggie Donnelly. 'She put this cap on my head and said, "What do you think?" And I said, "That's Liam for sure." The cap says "Gunk Clear", which is a proprietary grease for cleaning engine parts and all sorts of mess. And with Liam and Donal around, there's usually plenty of mess to clear up.'

Another money-making scheme – Liam and Donal carry the statue of Our Lady of the Motherlode to their gold-panning tourist trap.

DONAL

played by FRANKIE McCAFFERTY

Donal gets dragged into all of Liam's plans.

'I was a Donal for a while,' admits Frankie McCafferty. 'When I left school, I didn't know what I wanted to do. I was in a band for a couple of years – my dad was a musician – and I worked on building sites and timber yards as part of the Irish government's training scheme. I spent one summer at a burger joint in the West End of London. So I can definitely identify with Donal.

'He's not as desperate as Liam to make money. He's not bothered about making anything of himself but he tags along for the ride. He does it for the fun, the craic – to him, any money is a bonus. When it comes to thinking about the consequences of Liam's various schemes, Donal can't see further than the end of his nose. He's much more superstitious and God-fearing than Liam, who can be quite cynical. In every respect of the word, he's a simple home-loving lad who's never going to leave BallyK.

'Liam and Donal are bringers of immediate madness. The moment you see them on screen, you think: "Here come Liam and Donal, here's trouble." Without doubt their success in the show is due to their lack of success…'

Thirty-one-year-old Frankie hails from Donegal, but it was in Galway where his acting career took off. 'I began acting at university for fun and in 1989 won a scholarship to go to drama school in Paris. My first major role was in a play called *Wild Harvest* at the Druid Theatre, Galway. I followed that up with the movie *Fools of Fortune* and then *Children of the North* for the BBC which starred Tony Doyle. I also worked with Dervla Kirwan when I was a stage manager at the Druid Theatre. She was seventeen and taking her final exams at school when she appeared in a play by Anthony Minghella, *A Little Like Drowning*.

'When I first read the general pitch for *Ballykissangel*, I have to admit that, being Irish, I didn't think it would work. And I hardly realised I'd auditioned for it! Joy Lale, Richard Standeven and Paul Harrison conducted this massive improvisation session at a hotel in Dublin. They'd give us certain situations, like trying to stop a loose horse running down the road, and ask us to improvise our actions. There must have been over thirty actors and it was such a fantastic laugh that I completely forgot it was work. In the end, I got offered the part without realising how big it was.'

The very nature of Donal's role means that Frankie has landed in a couple of scrapes on the show. 'When I was smuggling a suitcase that may or may not have contained human bones, I had to be nearly run over by a car. Our specialist driver, Reggie Blain, just drove the car extremely fast and told me to ignore him. It was easy to say, but I trusted him and it was fine. There was also the business when I had to fight Edso (played by Anthony Brophy) over the dumping of a pile of manure next to his caravan. The first take we did was pretty easy-going because Anthony's much bigger than me, but Richard Standeven wanted more action and said: "Really fight him, Frankie." Anthony was supposed to knock me over after a struggle but I fought so hard that he couldn't get me to the floor and I ended up knocking him down instead. Although it had all gone wrong, I was kind of chuffed about it. All my days of brawling in dance halls paid off…'

Donal poses as a professor to persuade tourists to part with their money.

EAMONN BYRNE

played by BIRDY SWEENEY

*Eccentric hill farmer
Eamonn Byrne.*

The scene called for eccentric old hill farmer Eamonn to sit on a donkey as part of Quigley's tourist film for Ballykissangel. 'I didn't think sitting on a donkey would be any problem at all,' says comedy veteran Birdy Sweeney, 'so I was surprised to see that they had got a stunt double in to play Eamonn. But the moment the stunt man sat on the donkey, it got very worked up and threw him off. I was glad I wasn't on it. The original idea was for Eamonn just to ride the donkey down the street, but the stunt man being tipped off looked so good that the director decided to keep it in!

'It just goes to show how unpredictable animals are – you should never try to be clever with them. But sometimes that can work in your favour. When we were doing the scenes up on the mountains with Eamonn and the inspector counting his sheep, the animals did exactly what we wanted them to. There was a line where the inspector said we were counting the same sheep twice and I said something like, "no, that one's got a limp". And right on cue, one sheep wandered into shot in front of the camera. We couldn't have scripted it better – the only thing that was missing was the limp!

'Every small rural community in Ireland has an Eamonn. He's a decent, hardworking, simple man who lives alone and treats his animals as his family. He loves his pigs, particularly Mary the sow, and keeps them happy by playing music to them. Times are hard for farmers like him and he's always trying to make ends meet, which is why he's forever on the lookout for EU subsidies. He thinks he's cunning, but the fact of it is you can see through him right away.'

Playing Eamonn takes sixty-five-year-old Birdy back to his own boyhood in Dungannon, County Tyrone. 'I came from a rural community – a minute from where I lived, I was in the heart of the country. As a boy I used to go in a horse and trap to a neighbour's farm and help with the hay, the horses and stacking turf. I had a clever old dog called Gypsy who used to go with me. The dog just used to lie down in the middle of the road because there was no traffic. It was a Ballykissangel setting, serene and quiet. So filming the show has brought back a lot of memories for me.'

Married with eight children (four boys and four girls), Birdy acquired his nickname from the bird impressions he used to do at school. 'Then when I went on to the stage, doing bird impressions was my first act before I moved on to comedy. I was a stand-up comedian for over thirty years but I didn't like the way comedians were becoming aggressive so I turned to drama, following in the footsteps of people like Max Wall. One of my first straight roles was as an extra in *Billy* with Kenneth Branagh, which was set in Northern Ireland, and then my stage drama debut was at the ripe old age of fifty-eight in *The Iceman Cometh* at The Abbey Theatre, Dublin. Drama has given me a new lease of life – in fact, I've had more success as an actor than I ever did as a comedian. I'm busier now than I've ever been. I must be like a fine wine – I improve with age.

Eamonn with his glamorous 'niece' Naomi.

'I somehow sensed I would get the part of Eamonn. I loved the character – I could almost feel him – and I was laughing out loud while reading the scripts. I said to my wife, "I'm sure I'm going to get this," and luckily I did. And the wonderful thing is that casting people are now asking for me. Such is the power of television.'

Despite his new career, Birdy has never managed to shake off his showbusiness origins entirely. 'Two years ago I played a character called Birdy Doyle in a play entitled *The Only True History of Lizzie Finn*. Like me, Birdy Doyle was a music-hall artist who did bird impressions. I said to the producers, "I no longer have my own teeth so I can't whistle now," but they said, "Don't worry, we'll use a backing tape." I wanted to give it a go though, so I tried making a whistling sound by putting my fingers in my mouth and, to my amazement, even without my own teeth, I produced a pretty good whistle. In fact, it was so good, we didn't need the tape after all. It's funny the things you can learn, even at my age.'

DR MICHAEL RYAN

played by BOSCO HOGAN

Bosco Hogan has been able to draw on a wealth of experience for his portrayal of Ballykissangel doctor Michael Ryan. 'I was born in Drogheda, County Louth, which is a very rural area like BallyK, so I had a good basic knowledge of country life. Also, the local doctor was a friend of my parents and was often at our house.

'And when I landed the part of Dr Ryan, I was able to consult my own Dublin GP who used to work in the country. He told me that a country doctor is almost an agony uncle in that he lends a sympathetic ear to his patients. In many ways he fulfils a similar function to a priest – the onus is on him to be discreet. My doctor has also helped me with various medical procedures – such as taking blood pressure and dealing with damaged limbs – because although I haven't had to deal with anything gory, just minor cuts and bruises, I still want it to look right. I don't want to be receiving letters of complaint from doctors, saying I'm not doing it properly. Besides my own research, our unit nurse Teresa Gantly is always on hand to keep us up to date with medical matters.'

Easy-going and approachable, Dr Ryan is a popular member of the Ballykissangel community. 'He's a very dedicated man,' says Bosco, 'who makes it his business to keep abreast of the latest technology. He's not a stick-in-the-mud GP. He is married, but we haven't seen his wife yet. Eagle-eyed viewers may remember an attractive woman accompanying him to Niamh's wedding, but she was played by an extra so I doubt she'll turn out to be Mrs Ryan. But I look forward to acquiring a wife.'

There are no such mysteries about Bosco's own family. He is married to Leslie and they have three children – Hugh, sixteen, Daragh, thirteen, and Niamh who is ten. The son of a distiller, Bosco was born forty-eight years ago, the third of six children. 'I am the only one who has gone into acting, although my sister Catherine is an announcer with RTE and also makes classical music programmes for radio. My other two sisters are a nurse and a teacher, while one brother is an architect, the other an engineer.

'I can remember the exact moment when I decided I wanted to be an actor – I was four years old, and I went to see a production of *The Pirates of Penzance*. I was fascinated by it, and then, when I was twelve, I played Jessica in the school play *The Merchant of Venice*. Funnily enough, my next role in a school play was also a girl – Celia in *As You Like It*. I had a high voice and youthful looks in those days.

Even when I was twenty-seven, I played a sixteen-year-old, but all that changed when I lost my hair!'

Instead of attending drama school, Bosco joined the RTE Radio Repertory Company. 'I was there for two years and it was a terrific learning experience, working with some fine actors in a wide range of parts. There's no training that's as good as working at the sharp end. After that I joined the Abbey Theatre, Dublin, but after four years there I decided that working with the same people every day was a bit too much like working in an office, so I left to go freelance.'

Since then he has appeared in countless productions, including *The Rockingham Shoot, The Chief* and a prestigious BBC production of *Dracula*. 'When my wife looked at the *Dracula* cast list and saw names like Frank Finlay, Louis Jourdan, Jack Shepherd and Susan Penhaligon, she said to me: "Yours is the only name I don't recognise!"'

Between 1977 and 1984 Bosco lived in London but returned to Ireland so that his children could go to school in Dublin. Away from *Ballykissangel*, he has his own one-man show on the poet W.B. Yeats, *I Am of Ireland,* which he has taken to Rome, London and the United States. He is also starring in a new RTE detective series, *Making the Cut.* 'I play Detective Inspector Gerry Cody, a tough disciplinarian who is addicted to mints. It's a nice contrast to Dr Ryan.'

Summoned by Donal, Dr Michael Ryan hurries to rescue the stricken Quigley.

KATHLEEN HENDLEY

played by AINE NI MHUIRI

Virtually everything about modern life shocks BallyK's moral guardian, shopkeeper Kathleen Hendley.

By no stretch of the imagination could shopkeeper Kathleen Hendley, the eyes and ears of Ballykissangel, be termed a regular at Fitzgerald's. Indeed, apart from one glass of sherry at Christmas, no alcohol ever passes her lips. But the widow Hendley is a key member of the community, if only because she sees herself as its moral guardian, opposing anything that smacks of fun, sex, drink, men, movies, music or literature. A religious zealot, she loathes Assumpta and strongly disapproves of Father Clifford's liberal approach, reporting any untoward behaviour by the young priest straight to Father Mac. At times she makes Mary Whitehouse look like one of the Spice Girls.

It is hard to imagine two more diverse personalities than the prim and proper Kathleen and actress Aine Ni Mhuiri, whose conversation is regularly punctuated with the sound of laughter. 'Kathleen's heart is in the right place,' says Aine, 'and she does try to do the right thing. It's just that she keeps jumping to the wrong conclusions. And of course she does look up to Father Mac, who can do no wrong in her eyes.

'Most villages have an anchor figure like Kathleen who has lived there for years and knows everyone's business. To me, the moment which summed her up perfectly was when she stepped straight out into the road and Father Clifford had to jam on the brakes in Assumpta's van. She stopped him and Assumpta dead with her look. How dare they nearly run her over! She thought she had the right of way. In fact, it was that episode by John Forte which has resulted in the character of Kathleen snowballing. It was only a very small part at first, and I think it's fair to say that Kieran Prendiville didn't envisage the character working. I particularly enjoyed the scene in series two where she had to play the organ in church. I thought it was typical of her to be the church organist and what's more, to be a bad church organist. I learned to play that piece but I hadn't really played the piano for years so, believe me, it wasn't difficult for me to play it badly!'

Dublin-born Aine, who has been married to teacher Noel for twenty-four years and has two teenage children, Eoin, sixteen, and Trersr, eighteen, has been acting since her twenties. 'I was very interested in the Irish Language Theatre and among the people I worked with there in the 1960s was Niall Toibin, who plays Father Mac. So we go back a long way. And in the past I've also worked with Tony Doyle and Deirdre Donnelly, so it was like a reunion on *Ballykissangel*.'

Aine's best-known role was Lily, the cleaner with the heart of gold, in the Dublin soap *Fair City*. 'I played Lily for seven years and only left the show to do *Ballykissangel*. I felt it was time to move on. Now children in the street don't know whether to call me Lily or Mrs Hendley.

'Working on *Ballykissangel* is a joy – there's such a lovely feeling to the show. One thing I did have to learn though, as a shopkeeper, was how to operate a cash register. Fortunately a friend of mine is a salesman for cash registers, so he lent me one to practise on. After all, I didn't want to get my hand trapped in it. Even now it's not that easy working the till and timing it with your lines. Luckily we don't see the till as much as we used to.'

Aine Ni Mhuiri and Niall Toibin talk through a scene with director of photography Colin Munn.

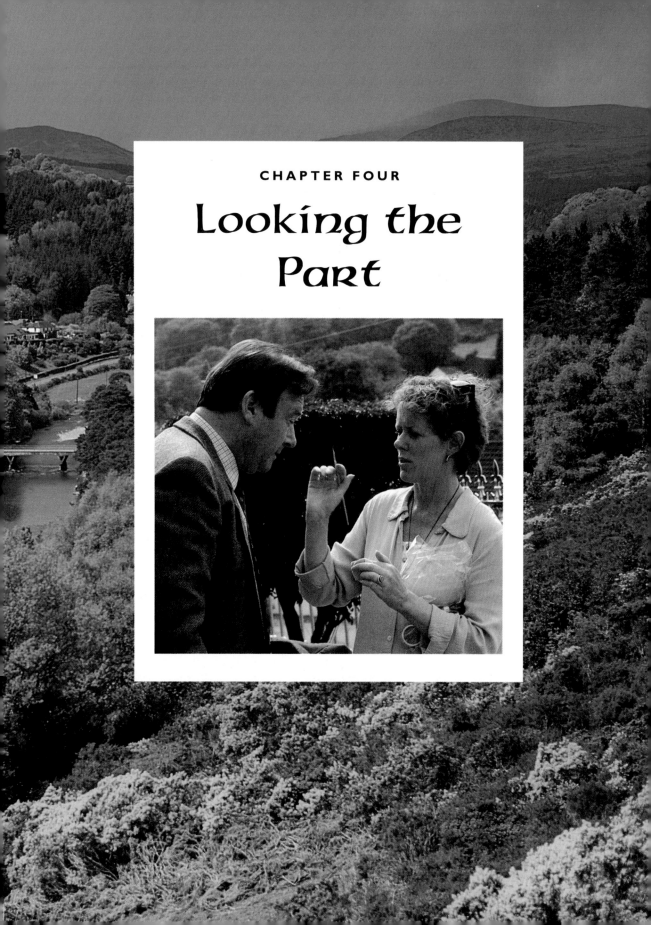

CHAPTER FOUR

Looking the Part

The first time Father Clifford was seen in clerical clothing in *Ballykissangel,* he was distinctly lacking in dignity. This wasn't simply because he was an awkward stranger in town, but more because he had a cut-up Fairy Liquid bottle wrapped around his neck.

Chief make-up artist Margot Wilson sets to work on Tina Kellegher between takes.

Costume designer Maggie Donnelly explains: 'We get our dog collars from a clerical shop in Dublin which also supplies us with vestments. On the first day of filming, we were taking the shirts out of their boxes and I went to look for Stephen's dog collar. But it wasn't there. I said to my assistant: "Where's his collar? Where's his collar?" Unfortunately, she had thought it was part of the inner packing of the shirt and had thrown it in the bin. With no spare, we had to improvise a dog collar out of a Fairy Liquid bottle. We've learned our lesson after that inauspicious start, and now I buy about fifty dog collars a year so that we've always got plenty around in case of emergencies.

'We use detachable dog collars because there are times – such as when he took his driving test – that Father Clifford likes to be incognito. Being a country priest, he doesn't have a lot of clothes and because his wages would not be astronomical, he wouldn't be able to afford immaculately fitted suits. In fact, Stephen's suits are deliberately bought in a size too small so that they're slightly tight on him and not a perfect fit. With wear and tear, he gets through about three a year – they get very shiny.

PREVIOUS PAGE The dapper Quigley (Tony Doyle) receives a few finishing touches from make-up assistant Joni Galvin.

'Since he and Father Mac are invariably dressed in black, I put the other characters in colours. I won't allow Assumpta to wear black because she is in so many scenes with Father Clifford. The smartest dresser is probably Quigley, who looks the part of the loud country gent with his checked shirts, except when the mad housekeeper came and put him in a blazer. None of the cast wear their own clothes. I buy a lot of second-hand clothes from places like Oxfam because I don't want the characters wearing new stuff – they wouldn't in real life. We also like to make as much as we can, particularly Dervla's skirts, because she likes a certain style which you can't always get. For Niamh's wedding, we made both Tina's dress and Dervla's bridesmaid's dress. Afterwards, we got letters from people wanting to know where they could get copies of the dresses for their own weddings.

'Where we have big crowd scenes, we give the extras a brief about what to wear. Obviously if they turn up not looking right, we change their outfits. We had to do a lot of dressing for the wedding scenes by adding hats here and there, because understandably not everyone had Sunday-best clothes. Recently we wanted all the local men to wear jackets for a church procession, but a lot said they didn't own a jacket, so again we had to supply the clothes. Most of the costumes on *Ballykissangel* are fairly straightforward, although we did have to rustle up a Santa costume for the Christmas special. It had to be worn by Liam, Donal and a third character who is a big drunk. Donal's very small so we made something which will look massive on him but really tight on the other guy.

'Niamh's pregnancy has also been a challenge. When Tina Kellegher played a pregnant girl in *The Snapper*, she had a special corset made for her bump. Tina

Hair assistant Una O'Sullivan attends to Dervla Kirwan.

loved it, so we got the woman who made it to produce another one for this pregnancy. It's a corset which is padded and layered with wadding and then a piece of stretch material is wrapped around the circumference to make it smooth. It's even got a belly button! And because Tina likes to feel the weight of the lump, we've put in fishing weights so that it feels like a six-pound bulge.'

The chief hairdresser on *Ballykissangel* is Eileen Doyle. 'Hair is such an important part in establishing a character,' says Eileen. 'You can tell so much about someone from their hair. For example, I changed Kathleen's style early on to make her look more definite, because she is quite a forceful character. And I always keep Father Mac's hair shiny and silver because it gives him an air of strength and authority and contrasts well with Father Clifford.

'Even in country villages the girls have nice hair, so Niamh and Assumpta always look pretty. And when we had the wedding, it was a real treat to be able to smarten up Siobhan for the day because she never gets the chance to look glamorous. I must say it's a wonderful show to work on because all of the cast are so lovely. They're almost like family.'

Chief make-up artist Margot Wilson was overjoyed when she heard that the Christmas show

Chief hairdresser Eileen Doyle prepares Tina Kellegher for a scene.

would include a mining accident. 'I've been secretly hoping for a mini-disaster in *Ballykissangel*,' she laughs, 'so that I can make some blood. Until now, it's just been the odd bruises and cuts, but the mining disaster required plenty of blood and dirt. It was great!

'We also had a burglar with a broken wrist in one episode of the new series, so I was able to build up his wrist to look swollen. Sadly the script made no mention of any bones sticking out, so I couldn't get to work with the chicken bones…

'For the regular cast, the make-up is fairly routine. Assumpta has the natural look of a country girl but we've had to make Niamh look a bit tired while she is pregnant. So we've given Tina Kellegher baggy eyes – she's very good about it, though.

'The most challenging character to do is probably old Eamonn. He has a wart on his face – made from tuboplast – and we have to make sure that Birdy Sweeney doesn't shave for a couple of days beforehand so that there's a good growth of stubble. Then we paint or stipple in a series of broken veins on his face and dirty him down, using a proprietary dirt with added gel. The overall effect suggests that he hasn't washed for a month. Birdy loves it!'

OPPOSITE Assumpta, Father Clifford and the unshaven Eamonn lead the protest for Brendan's reinstatement.

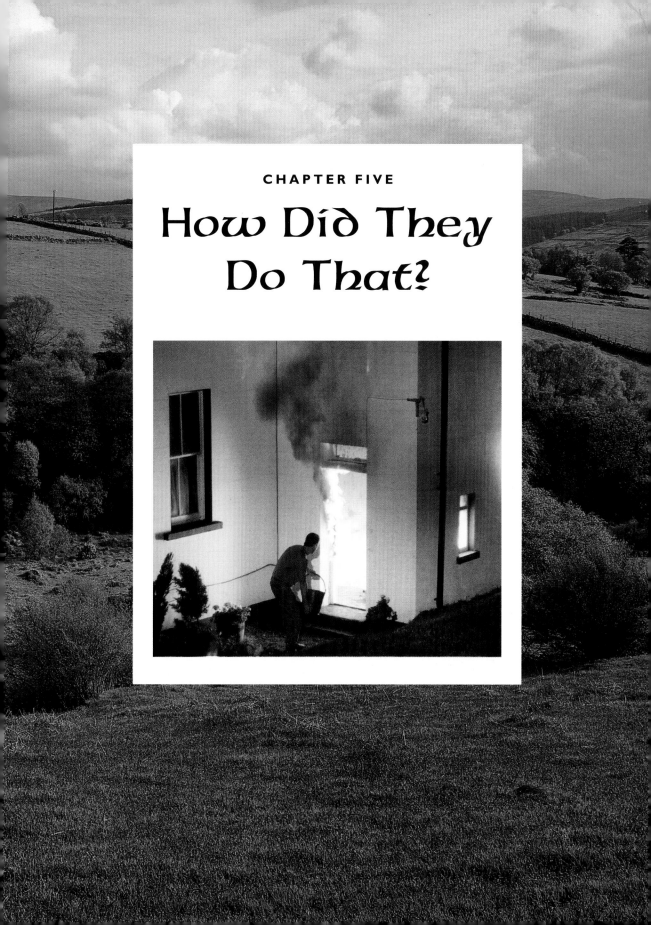

CHAPTER FIVE

How Did They Do That?

The opening to the very first episode of *Ballykissangel*, which was directed by Richard Standeven, involved a spectacularly quirky stunt which immediately established the style of the show and hooked the audience straight away. It was, of course, the sight of Quigley's imported confessional box tumbling down the mountainside right in front of the bus bearing the newly arrived Father Clifford. The scene was filmed up on Lugnaquilla, Wicklow's highest peak, and was almost as hair-raising as it appeared on screen.

The first test confessional boxes were just crates made of balsa wood and when they were rehearsed being tipped off the back of the lorry and down the mountain, they just blew away, scattered and smashed into thousands of pieces. So that idea was scrapped, and instead a strong metal cage was built to fit inside the box and the box itself was given a heavy frame to make it more stable. The sheer weight also made it potentially lethal and when it came hurtling 200 feet down the hill towards the bus that Reggie Blain was driving, it barely missed the bus. If the box had hit the bus, it would undoubtedly have knocked it off the road. The box had to be released from a great height and travel at great speed because it was meant to jump the road on which the bus was travelling. Although the scene was shot on a private road, there were no tricks as such – it was just a wonderful piece of driving…and luck.

Paul Harrison, who, along with Dermot Boyd, has directed most of the episodes to date, says: 'Lugnaquilla is very beautiful, but also very wild. The winds up there can be ferocious. We also filmed on Lugnaquilla for the story where Quigley met up with his old girlfriend. We built the hut where they were to have their rendezvous on the top of the mountain, but we got hit by the most horrendous winds that night. Only the fact that ten people and a pile of camera equipment were inside kept the hut on the ground, but we nearly lost the hut, the camera, everything, before we eventually decided to abandon filming for the night. Otherwise, out of a ten-week shoot on the first series, I had just three days of rain. We were blessed! Nobody filming in Ireland has such good weather! And we even used one of the wet days to good effect. It was where Assumpta was teaching Father Clifford to drive and he nearly ran over Kathleen as she crossed the road. The pouring rain made the scene more dramatic.'

Aine Ni Mhuiri, who plays Kathleen, wasn't sorry when that particular scene was over. 'I was a bit wary, but our stunt coordinator Philippe Zone worked everything out meticulously and took me through it, telling me exactly how many steps I had to take out into the road. And there was a double driving the van. Even so, I was quite relieved that we only had to do it once.'

Stephen had reason to be grateful to Philippe Zone when he found himself hanging from a window ledge of the church in the second series. Stephen says:

'I had to open the window and two pigeons flew out, causing me to let go of the ladder. I then had to hold on by one arm. What the viewers couldn't see was Philippe on the inside grabbing hold of my wrist for dear life. There was a drop of 15 feet so I was rather glad he didn't let go.'

One of the most dramatic scenes was the burning down of Kathleen's house. Even the immensely helpful folk of Avoca draw the line at allowing their home to be razed to the ground, so an alternative plan had to be drawn up. Designer David Wilson reveals: 'We staged the fire by adding on a large section to the back of Hendley's shop in Avoca. Kathleen lives underneath at the back of the shop, as do the real Hendley family, and since we couldn't exactly burn their house down, I built a fake side on to the house and it was that which we set fire to. Special effects achieved the fire with controllable propane gas jets, the sort they use on *London's Burning*. Then we built the interior of the burned-out section and the refurbished rooms in the studio. The house itself was completely undamaged, although the family couldn't see out of that side of the building for six weeks because we had blocked off all the windows. They were very patient, though.'

Hendley's shop in Avoca, situated opposite Fitzgerald's.

Among Peter Hanly's favourite moments was the scene where Ambrose found God after the head of the statue crashed through the roof of his car. Paul Harrison explains how it was done: 'We built a scaffold right up to the top of the church and rigged a system of pulleys. We had six different weights of head — some very light, which we could manhandle, and some very heavy. They were all made of polystyrene, but wood was added to some of the bases to make them heavier. We put a fake roof in Ambrose's car, had a really heavy head made up and dropped it in from ten feet, not right from the top. We had measured it to the inch so that it would go through the dummy roof but, even though we had a spare roof, it was essential to get the angle of the drop spot-on. I'm proud to say we got it in one. What you saw on screen was a lighter head being dropped from the top of the church and then we cut to a heavy one halfway down.

One of the most spectacular scenes from the second series was the fire which badly damaged Kathleen's house.

'The crowning of the ram ceremony, where the animal was raised to the top of a tower of scaffolding, was a particularly fraught affair, not because of the ram but because our director of photography had to dash home to attend to a personal crisis. We had to fly out a replacement on the actual night of the shoot, which was tricky because he didn't know any of us and wasn't used to the show.

Producer Chris Griffin, director Paul Harrison and director of photography John Record.

It was very tight, but he pulled through and so did the ram. The ram was brilliant. As Father Clifford said in the programme, the ram might as well be up that tower as up a mountain. He had a nice comfy box to stand in and we didn't leave him up there long. All in all, he was a very happy ram. Stephen was OK climbing the scaffold, but Deirdre Donnelly had a harness, to be on the safe side.'

But one incident from *Ballykissangel* was more reminiscent of an episode from *The X Files*. Paul Harrison says: 'It happened in the scene where we replaced the statue at the top of the church. We had to lift Stephen and Niall Toibin 60 feet up into the air on a "cherry-picker" (like a fireman's hydraulic platform) to get them on a platform which was just ten feet square. It was an uncomfortable scene, anyway. Niall has no head for heights, and with the church at Avoca standing on a hill looking over the valley, it felt even higher. But the curious thing was that after finally completing the scene, we found that the film was ruined. The negative had an extraordinary orange glow emanating from the bottom of the film up, and nobody could explain where this mystery colour was coming from. Usually there's a technician around who can come up with the answer to any filming phenomenon, but on this occasion nobody had an explanation. Personally, I think we were pushing our luck with two priests up there! We ended up having to rebuild the church spire on scaffolding six weeks later in the garden of Quigley's house at Enniskerry and re-shooting it there. This time the film was fine, but the whole episode was decidedly spooky.'

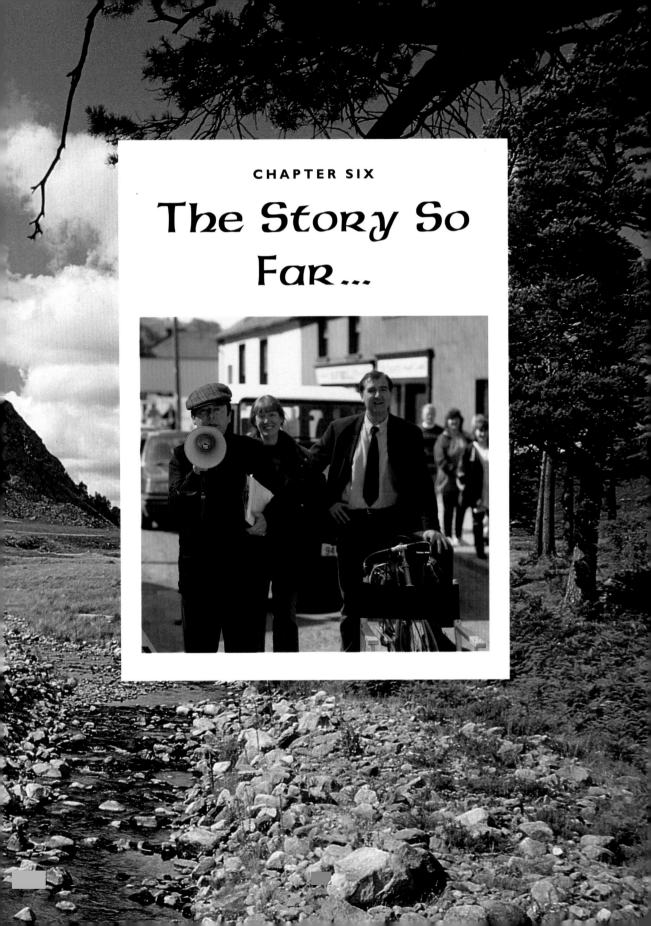

CHAPTER SIX

The Story So Far...

Trying To Connect You

writer: Kieran Prendiville

director: Richard Standeven

transmission date: 11 February 1996

PREVIOUS PAGE *Brian Quigley, the Quentin Tarantino of Ballykissangel, directs filming in the main street, holding up the traffic in the process.*

After a close encounter with a falling confessional box which tumbles down the mountain in front of the Ballykissangel bus, Father Peter Clifford decides to walk the last few miles to his new posting. But a van pulls up and Assumpta Fitzgerald offers him a lift. When he explains who he is and that he is starting work at St Joseph's, her sarcastic reaction leaves little room for misinterpretation: 'One thing this country needs is priests from England.'

Father Clifford's arrival is closely followed by that of the recovered confessional box, a state-of-the-art contraption boasting electrically-operated doors, air conditioning and a fax machine. It has been donated to St Joseph's by the entrepreneurial Brian Quigley, who hopes it will lead to lucrative orders from other churches. A minor complication is that it has to be lowered through the roof. Father Clifford protests to Father MacAnally that it is an unnecessary extravagance, but is told that he should not look a gift horse in the mouth. He is also told that he will have to get some form of transport as his parishioners are scattered around the countryside.

Quigley's daughter Niamh seeks Father Clifford's advice. She wants her boyfriend Ambrose, the local Gard, to agree to a trial marriage to find out whether they'll get on, but Ambrose thinks it would be immoral. Later in the new confessional, Ambrose puts his point of view and Father Clifford suggests a compromise – live together and share everything except sex. Then something emerges from the fax machine: a huge bill for the confessional from the manufacturers in Italy.

That night, Father Clifford receives an urgent summons to give the last rites to a dying man who lives on the mountain, but with no transport, he asks Assumpta to take him in her van. They arrive too late – the man died ten minutes earlier. Father Clifford is deeply distressed.

> FATHER CLIFFORD (contemplating buying a 50cc motorbike): *If I can ride a bike, I can ride one of these, surely?*
>
> PADRAIG: *I was thinking of your dignity.*
>
> FATHER CLIFFORD: *Jesus entered Jerusalem on a donkey.*
>
> PADRAIG: *He'd have been quicker.*

At Sunday Mass, Father Clifford publicly decries the high-tech confessional and when he receives a final demand on the fax machine, he decides to deliver the bill, intended for Quigley, to the Bishop in Cilldargan. Father Mac is hauled over the coals and has to tell Quigley to get rid of the confessional. 'He wants it out, Brian, and, if I quote him correctly, "before that chancer Quigley puts advertising on the doors"!'

Niamh moves in with Ambrose, angering Quigley, who thinks that Father Clifford has encouraged the unholy arrangement. He bursts into the confessional to confront the priest, but the door jams and both are trapped inside as it is winched into the air through the church roof.

> FATHER CLIFFORD: *Where am I, Assumpta? The Twilight Zone?*
> ASSUMPTA: *No, Father, you're just out of your depth.*

Arriving in Ballykissangel proves something of a culture shock for Father Clifford.

The Things We Do For Love

writer: Kieran Prendiville

director: Richard Standeven

transmission date: 18 February 1996

Jenny Clarke, a young parishioner of Father Clifford's when he was in Manchester, arrives in Ballykissangel and checks into Fitzgerald's, telling Assumpta she has 'come for the priest'.

At confession, local vet Siobhan Mehigan relates how she got so drunk the previous evening that she woke up in a field full of sheep. Father Clifford hands her a couple of aspirins and, out of gratitude, she gives him a hot racing tip. Father Clifford has also been playing in goal for the local Gaelic football team, who are practising hard for a needle match with Cilldargan, until a rough tackle injures his ribs. At Dr Michael Ryan's surgery, Father Clifford hears about a young couple with a sick baby whose lives are being made difficult by Quigley. The latter wants to develop holiday homes, but the couple's caravan is parked on the land and so he wants them out of the way. To hasten their departure, he got his men, Liam and Donal, to dump manure a few yards from their window. Father Clifford arrives at the caravan just as another load is about to be dumped. When Edso, the baby's father, starts to fight Liam and Donal, Father Clifford tries to intervene but ends up right in the manure.

> SIOBHAN (in confession): *Will you let me do something for you – a small contribution to the missions?*
> FATHER CLIFFORD: *Of course.*
> SIOBHAN: *In the 8.15 at Fairyhouse, Roxy's Cracker should go very close.*

Father Clifford has another surprise when he gets home – Jenny is waiting for him. She embarrasses him by talking about the 'special relationship' they had in Manchester and prepares a candlelit supper, a scene witnessed by Kathleen Hendley, resident shopkeeper and killjoy. While Jenny goes upstairs to his bedroom, Father Clifford sneaks out and stays the night at Fitzgerald's. Later he admits that he did have feelings for her in Manchester…and that was why he had asked for a transfer.

Edso repays Quigley by depositing a pile of manure on his doorstep. Quigley accompanies Liam and Donal on the dumper truck, ready to return the compliment, but Father Clifford is tipped off and turns up in time to confront them. He challenges them to dump it on him. They back off.

After her initial hostility towards him, Assumpta begins to see another side to Father Clifford. But she can never quite separate the man from his vocation.

Father Mac demands an explanation for what Kathleen saw the previous night but Father Clifford assures him that it was all perfectly innocent. When Father Clifford rallies by complaining about Quigley's behaviour in terrorising Edso's family, Father Mac reveals that it is Assumpta, not Quigley, who owns the field where the caravanners are squatting. Assumpta in turn says that she had merely asked Liam and Donal to 'use their initiative' to move the family on so that she could sell the land to Quigley. She had even offered them money but they had rejected it, because it wasn't enough to put down as a deposit on a home of their own.

Come the day of the football match and Father Clifford has been selected as reserve for BallyK. Siobhan is confident of a Cilldargan victory, so Father Clifford suggests to Assumpta that she puts the money she offered to Edso on Cilldargan. Edso is Cilldargan's star player. Injury to BallyK's regular goalkeeper forces Father Clifford into the action and, in view of the bet, Assumpta assumes that he'll throw the match. But he tries his hardest, only to be beaten by a twice-taken penalty. Edso now has enough money for his house deposit.

Father Clifford and Jenny say their farewells, her parting shot being: 'You'll know the next time.' He knows he must make sure there is no next time.

FATHER CLIFFORD (explaining himself): *I went to Fitzgerald's. An old friend turned up unexpectedly. I couldn't turn her out in the pouring rain, so I turned myself out. The only woman I spent the night with was Assumpta Fitzgerald...It was a joke.*
FATHER MAC: *Father, that kind of joke stopped being funny in this country when everyone realised it was actually happening.*

Live In My Heart And Pay No Rent

writer: Kieran Prendiville

director: Paul Harrison

transmission date: 25 February 1996

Niamh is preparing for her wedding to Ambrose, but as the Gard leaves St Joseph's, the stone head of a saint falls from the roof of the church and crashes down onto his car a split second after he had got out. Believing it to be the head of St John the Evangelist, patron saint of priests, he sees it as a sign from heaven and calls off the wedding, declaring his intention of joining the priesthood instead.

Hill farmer Eamonn Byrne is having to show a government official concrete evidence of the number of sheep he is claiming Euro subsidies for – sheep which seem strangely elusive as the two men tramp around the mountainside. Later, in the pub, when Padraig O'Kelly suggests the authorities might be using a satellite which can track sheep, Eamonn realises he has to act fast if he's going to pull the wool over their eyes.

Quigley is planning to meet up again with Rosarie, an old girlfriend. They split up when he fell in love with Niamh's mother but not before vowing to meet up again in twenty-five years' time at the top of their favourite mountain, to see if they still felt the same way about each other. Liam and Donal are instructed to build a mountain-top hut ready for the rendezvous.

EAMONN (counting his sheep): *There's one.*

GOVERNMENT OFFICIAL: *We've already counted that one.*

EAMONN: *Ah no look, that fella has a limp.*

GOVERNMENT OFFICIAL: *Tired himself out.*

EAMONN: *What?*

GOVERNMENT OFFICIAL: *Trying to be in so many places at once.*

Heartbroken at being jilted, Niamh insists on holding a 'Hardly a Wedding Reception' at Fitzgerald's, an event fuelled by fresh supplies of stout from the brewery. Assumpta had cancelled the order but a desperate rep provides her with free booze to keep the honourable Irish drinking tradition alive. Assumpta sells it at the reception and puts the proceeds to one side. But it needs more than a few drinks to cheer up Niamh. Assumpta blames Father Clifford for Ambrose's sudden calling and tells him to do something about it…lie if necessary. So he does, telling Ambrose that the stone head which just missed him was St John the Baptist, not the

Evangelist. Seeing the error of his ways, Ambrose gatecrashes the reception and asks Niamh to marry him, resulting in widespread celebrations and even greater consumption of the black stuff.

Up on the mountain, Rosarie has a present for Quigley – a punch on the jaw for deserting her all those years ago. They spend the night chatting before she returns to her husband. On their way down, they admire the view, including Eamonn's masterplan to fool the satellite – wooden sheep.

Father Mac is disappointed that the Church has lost a potential priest in Ambrose, but Assumpta is delighted and hands Father Clifford the cash from the sales of the free stout to go towards repairing the church roof. 'Ambrose isn't a priest,' Father Clifford explains to his boss. 'He's a policeman – natural born, cold-hearted, ruthless.' At that moment Father Mac looks out of the window and sees Ambrose supervising the towing away of his car…

> AMBROSE (considering the benefits of marriage): *'Tis a lonesome wash doesn't have a man's shirt in it, right enough.*

When Ambrose finds God, he calls off the wedding. However, he and Niamh are reunited thanks to the intervention of Father Clifford.

Fallen Angel

writer: John Forte

director: Paul Harrison

transmission date: 3 March 1996

'Coming live from somewhere near you' is a pirate radio station, Angel FM. The DJ is clearly someone in the midst of the BallyK community – he even knows it is Father Clifford's birthday – and when Ambrose finds himself humiliated over the airwaves, he determines to seek out the mystery broadcaster.

> ASSUMPTA (about Michael Bradley):
>
> *He has two things which always interest the Church: money and no next of kin.*

During a hospital visit, Father Clifford meets the terminally ill Michael Bradley, a former judge with no friends or family. The priest wants to help but soon discovers that Bradley is hostile towards the Church. Father Mac admits that he never saw eye to eye with Bradley but, more to the point, warns Father Clifford that if he doesn't learn to drive, his job could be in jeopardy. 'BallyK needs a four-wheeled priest.' Assumpta organises a surprise birthday party for Father Clifford, at which she hands him a voucher entitling him to six free driving lessons, to be given by her. On their first outing, he is just telling Assumpta that observation let him down on his test when he fails to spot Kathleen step out into the road. At least he knows how to execute an emergency stop. Assumpta tells him he has nothing to worry about. 'No priest has ever failed the test round here – it's a perk.'

Father Clifford manages to establish a rapport with Bradley over a game of chess, although the old man warns him: 'I enjoy sacrificing bishops'. Bradley confesses that he helped his wife to die by administering morphine when she was suffering great pain. Father Clifford is shocked by the revelation and seeks advice from Father Mac, who merely tells him that he has fixed (in more ways than one) his driving test for Thursday. He tells his curate to make sure he is wearing his dog collar for the test. Realising what Assumpta said is true, Father Clifford resolves to pass the test on merit and removes his collar before the examiner appears. He ends up passing with flying colours.

With Donal posing as a satisfied customer, Quigley is doing radio advertisements to promote his new holiday homes development. When the commercial goes out on Angel FM, Ambrose steps up his search and acquires a detector. He finally tracks down the transmitter in the storeroom of Kathleen's shop where the DJ turns out to be her seventeen-year-old nephew Daniel. Ambrose is bent on prosecution, but Father Clifford persuades him to let the lad provide a radio service for the hospital. When Father Clifford calls at the hospital, he learns that Bradley has died. He wouldn't take the last rites from Father Mac – he had wanted to see Father Clifford, but he was out taking his driving test. The ward sister hands Father Clifford a set of car keys – a gift from Bradley. They belong to a fine vintage car. His job is safe.

KATHLEEN: *Do you know sloth is a sin?*

DANIEL: *An' I thought it was a hairy mammal.*

Father Clifford and Father Mac disagreed over Michael Bradley.

The Power And The Gory

writer: John Forte

director: Paul Harrison

transmission date: 10 March 1996

Following the death of 'Big Bertie' O'Doyle, the local Dail member, Father Mac tries to persuade Quigley to stand for election against Sean Dooley, 'plumber, councillor and anti-Christ'. After feigning indifference to the suggestion, Quigley appears in the main street, his car emblazoned with election posters, and conducts a very public row with Dooley over the megaphones.

In an uncustomary display of generosity, Quigley pays for the discordant church bell of St Joseph's to be replaced. Father Clifford suspects there is an ulterior motive, but Father Mac is quite happy with the arrangement. Then Quigley reveals that the new full peal is, in fact, a tape of the bells of Galway Cathedral, and soon he is relaying his election message over the church's broadcasting system. Quigley is also in Niamh's bad books for pleading poverty whenever she mentions the wedding reception.

> FATHER CLIFFORD (watching Assumpta climb a ladder up the side of the church): *What are you doing? You can't go up there.*
>
> ASSUMPTA: *You should be pleased, Father. This is the nearest I've been to God in years.*

The by-election is being covered by a television crew, the reporter for which is Leo McGarvey, an old boyfriend of Assumpta's. He is keen to win her back and confesses his feelings to Father Clifford, although he thinks she is interested in someone else. Father Clifford remains impartial and advises Leo to talk to her frankly. When she finds out that the two men have been talking about her, Assumpta hits the roof.

Meanwhile, a skeleton from the past threatens to wreck Quigley's campaign. It has been found on a building site belonging to Quigley and is thought to be that of a local hermit, Tommy McIvor, known to all as 'one-tooth Tommy'. Quigley's immediate concerns are that no one will want to live over the bones of the dead and that work on the site might be halted pending an investigation. So he decides to keep it quiet. However, Leo finds out and he and his camera crew follow Quigley with the remains to the church, but Quigley lays a false trail to outwit his pursuer. Ambrose points out that Quigley committed an offence in unlawfully

removing the 'body' but, in mitigation, Father Clifford points out that Quigley has had a lot on his mind, what with the election and his daughter's forthcoming wedding. Indeed, the priest suggests that there is little point in delaying the wedding any longer. Ambrose agrees wholeheartedly and Quigley is left with little option but to go along with it. Father Clifford inters the bones with full burial rites.

Dooley wins the election and Quigley and Father Mac reveal that they both voted for him, to ensure he got shipped off to Dublin. Leo realises he's wasting his time chasing Assumpta and leaves alone, but not before implying that it is Father Clifford she cares for. She makes no attempt to deny it.

The loving relationship between Niamh and her father is jeopardised when he tells her he can't afford to pay for her and Ambrose's wedding reception.

Missing You Already

writer: Kieran Prendiville

director: Paul Harrison

transmission date: 17 March 1996

Father Mac informs Father Clifford that he must leave St Joseph's to return to England, implying that the locals won't miss him. That feeling appears to be confirmed when, as he is passing Fitzgerald's, a bucket of water is thrown over him. It is Assumpta's way of dealing with a burst pipe. When he tells her that he is being sent home, she appears disinterested but passes the information on to her regulars.

In a bid to attract tourists to a forthcoming festival in BallyK, Quigley decides to adapt a ceremony in Kerry where a goat is crowned, by doing something similar with a sheep. Padraig points out that it's plagiarism, but Assumpta doubts whether the goat will sue. However, Siobhan voices her disapproval as the unfortunate creature is hoisted in a crate up a scaffolding tower. Quigley has two other wheezes – a publicans' race through the village carrying trays of stout and his own temporary bar for the three-day festival, which would take lucrative business from Assumpta.

Quigley's Bar and Grill is soon up and running, and Assumpta can only watch in dismay as many of her regulars desert her. Needing some time alone, she pays a rare visit to St Joseph's. Father Clifford leaves her to it, but by the time he returns, Assumpta has gone and vandals have broken one of the windows. Father Clifford marches to Fitzgerald's to admonish Assumpta for not waiting for him to lock up, but is saddened to find that she has been hurt by the stone which smashed the window. Tenderly, he dresses her wound.

In the middle of the night Father Clifford is woken by the noise of a drunken Siobhan ascending the scaffold to release the ram. He climbs the scaffolding, urging her to come down, but finishes up helping her to lower the crate to the ground. After the animal has been released into the countryside, Father Clifford catches sight of Eamonn's wooden sheep and decides to substitute one for Quigley's ram. So when amidst much pomp and ceremony, Quigley has the crate lowered in readiness for the crowning, he is beside himself with anger at being the victim of a ram-raid.

Following Niamh and Ambrose's wedding, Quigley and Assumpta compete in the publicans' race. The winner gets to keep their bar open for the duration of the festival; the loser has to close. Assumpta wins, but Quigley isn't bothered – he says that the ever-vigilant Ambrose had closed his bar down anyway for breach of fire regulations. But Father Clifford has the last laugh, demonstrating how he had stuck down the glasses on Assumpta's tray. Assumpta shows Father Clifford a petition signed by the villagers demanding that he should stay on at St Joseph's. He quickly scans the list to see whether her name is there. He is not disappointed.

Always willing to lend a hand, Father Clifford sees his popularity confirmed by the petition urging him to stay at St Joseph's.

For One Night Only

writer: Kieran Prendiville

director: Paul Harrison

transmission date: 5 January 1997

It is the day of Ballykissangel's annual Charity Slave Auction where folk bid to buy each other's services for three hours, all in a good cause. Assumpta buys Father Clifford for £20 and soon has him working behind the bar, but she in turn is somewhat alarmed to find herself enslaved to Father Mac. However, her embarrassment pales into comparison with that of Brian Quigley, who fetches a mere £1 when bought by Liam. And Liam knows exactly what he's got in mind for his boss – unblocking drains. Revenge is sweeter than the smell of Quigley's clothes.

Niamh wants to buy Assumpta a present with a difference – former rock star Enda Sullivan, who has moved into the village. But Assumpta is distinctly

Crowds gather for the Ballykissangel Slave Auction.

unimpressed, dismissing Enda and his band Dark Rosaleen as 'one hit wonders back in the 80s'. Niamh can't hide her dismay. 'Honest to God, you'd think I'd walked in with Little Jimmy Osmond, the way she looked at him.' Enda is desperate for work and is hoping for a few gigs at Fitzgerald's. Assumpta tells him he'll have to audition. Meanwhile she finally discovers why Father Mac was so keen to buy her at the auction – he wants her to put up a bishop and two priests who are on a golfing holiday. Assumpta is appalled at the prospect of having three clergymen under her roof, but Father Clifford persuades her to agree to let the rooms.

A disapproving Father Mac watches with Brendan and Padraig as Father Clifford and Assumpta grow ever closer on stage during the play rehearsals.

Father Clifford has an ulterior motive. He has been coerced into directing 'Ryan's Mother: the prequel', a play claimed by Padraig as his own. Brendan advises the Father against any involvement, insisting that the play is dire. 'If it was a fight, you'd stop it,' he says. 'If it was a lame horse, you'd put it out of its misery.' It transpires that Brendan and Padraig had started work on the play together before going their separate ways. After mutual accusations of plagiarism, they settle their differences and opt for co-authorship. And Quigley agrees to sponsor the play, provided Father Clifford can get Assumpta to accommodate the clergy.

Assumpta and Enda are chosen to play the leads, but Assumpta is none too keen on some of the more passionate scenes. 'He doesn't have to be so close,' she protests. ''Course he does,' says Padraig. 'Where'd you expect him to play it from – Kilkenny?' But disaster strikes when Enda twists his ankle, forcing Father Clifford to take his place. The kissing scene with Assumpta is full of promise, until she pulls away, complaining about the lack of privacy in rehearsal. 'What are you going to do on the opening night?' demands Brendan. 'Ask the audience to wait outside?' With the hall cleared, she finally prepares to go through with the kiss.

'Assumpta,' says Father Clifford, glancing at the back of the hall.

'Don't,' she says, moving in to kiss him. 'We have to finish it.'

'I don't think so…'

'Why not?'

'Because standing at the back of the hall are Father Mac, two parish priests and a bishop.'

The bishop had checked out of Fitzgerald's, disappointed that his room had no TV or mini bar.

Thanks to the healing hands of Dr Ryan, Enda recovers just in time to make the first night. Father Clifford tries hard to hide his disappointment.

River Dance

writer: Kieran Prendiville

director: Paul Harrison

transmission date: 12 January 1997

Ballykissangel National School has to lose a teacher because of falling pupil numbers and on a 'last in, first out' basis, the unfortunate person is Brendan. Father Clifford and the rest of the villagers are up in arms, all the more so when it emerges that the man behind the decision was Father Mac, who disapproves of Brendan's liberal religious views. Father Clifford has other things on his mind, too – he is concerned about one of his parishioners, Mairie Kilfeather, who is being beaten by her husband Jimmy. Dr Ryan knows all about it, but is powerless to act.

When Liam and Donal see Enda Sullivan panning for gold in the river, they think there could be money to be made. They set up a tacky riverside shrine to 'Our Lady of the Motherlode', the statue coming complete with a glowing, battery-operated heart. They buy gold panning equipment and plan to turn the spot into a tourist attraction, making use of the fact that Timmy Joe Galvin drives the tourist bus. Timmy Joe duly delivers the tourists, who are met by Donal, posing as a professor to lecture them on the legend of gold in 'them there waters'.

Niamh and Ambrose are trying desperately for a baby and, much to the amusement of the pub regulars, Ambrose is called upon to 'do his duty' at any time of day. So when she finally announces that she is pregnant, Ambrose's joy is tinged with relief. He goes round the village walking on air, even allowing drivers to park illegally.

Assumpta leads a silent protest to Father Mac's in support of Brendan. To Father Mac's horror, Father Clifford joins the protesters. Back at St Joseph's, Mairie confesses to Father Clifford that, following another attack, she retaliated by hitting Jimmy with a frying pan, maybe fatally. Tipped off that a drunken Jimmy was heading for home, Ambrose goes to the Kilfeather house and follows a trail of blood to the river. There he finds Jimmy, unconscious but still breathing.

Brendan gets chatting to Enda, who reveals that he wants his eleven-year-old son to attend the local school. That one extra pupil means that Brendan's job is safe. Not such good news for Liam and Donal. Business has slumped to such an extent that they are obliged to sell their equipment at a loss to Quigley. Combing the river, Enda finds Jimmy's gold tooth.

OPPOSITE *Father Clifford expresses concern that Liam and Donal's flashing statue might be in dubious taste.*

In The Can

writer: John Forte

director: Paul Harrison

transmission date: 19 January 1997

Enda Sullivan plays at the folk Mass.

With Liam and Donal as his crew, Quigley decides to make a tourist film advertising Ballykissangel. Since the film is supposed to represent a view of rural Ireland which will appeal to Americans, Quigley gets Eamonn to dress suitably 'Oirish' and to ride a donkey down the main street. But the donkey has other ideas and tips Eamonn off. Filming moves on to Kathleen's shop where she is struggling to read her words. 'No wonder they're called idiot boards,' sighs an exasperated Quigley. He then tries to film Siobhan at work delivering a calf, only for soundman Donal to faint at the first sight of blood.

The pregnant Niamh has developed food cravings, including a passion for pickled onions. To make matters worse, she forces her diet on Ambrose, who is alarmed to be served porridge for lunch. She is also keen to pair off Assumpta and Enda and is delighted when the two go on a dinner date. Enda's friend Aileen is less pleased and refuses to babysit his son Feargal. The boy is meant to spend the evening at Padraig's house but runs home to await his father's return, thereby cutting short the date. Aileen seeks the advice of Father Clifford – it is clear that she and Enda are more than just friends. Father Clifford agrees to have a word with Enda, but he tells him to mind his own business. Feargal, however, has other ideas, and tells Assumpta about Aileen and his father. She is not sure whether to believe him, but puts Enda off when he asks for another date. When Quigley films Enda singing, he unwittingly captures on film a moment of intimacy between Enda and Aileen. The kiss is later witnessed by Niamh as she watches the video. She feels she ought to warn Assumpta and gives her the video.

Meanwhile Father Clifford has persuaded Enda to play the guitar at a special Sunday Mass aimed at young people. Father Mac is sceptical ('what's wrong with Kathleen on the organ?'), but is won over when told that it could be good for the collection. He agrees 'on one condition – that you don't sing "Michael, Row the Boat Ashore". I can't stand it.' The Mass is a great success – 'Michael, Row the Boat Ashore' included – although Donal fails to record any sound on the film. At Fitzgerald's, Assumpta watches Niamh's video. It is all over between her and Enda.

The Facts Of Life

writer: John Forte

director: Paul Harrison

transmission date: 26 January 1997

A new-born baby is left on Father Clifford's doorstep one night. With the help of Dr Ryan and Assumpta, he looks after the baby until it is taken off to hospital in Cilldargan. The incident inspires Father Clifford to give a talk on relationships to the youth club, a speech which the regulars in Fitzgerald's dub his 'sex talk'. He asks Kathleen whether she has any films which he could use as illustrations in the video section of her shop. Misunderstanding his request, Kathleen is appalled.

Baby talk is high on the agenda at the Egans' too, Ambrose announcing that if Niamh has a daughter, he wants her named after one of the Nolans. The thought leaves him so ecstatic that, on stepping out of the bath, he quite forgets himself and slips on the soap. While Ambrose is confined to bed, Superintendent Foley says he will bring in a temporary replacement – Gard McMullen, fresh out of training. Quigley is quick to take advantage of Ambrose's enforced absence and starts plans to transport topsoil from the hillside – selling a little bit of Ireland to the Irish. To ship the soil, he hires an enormous truck, one that is illegal on the narrow local roads.

> QUIGLEY (about Gard McMullen):
> *BallyK's his first assignment, is it?*
> SUPERINTENDENT FOLEY: *He's a very capable Garda.*
> QUIGLEY: *That will be a first.*

Tragically, Niamh miscarries. As she grieves at home with Ambrose, they are interrupted by the fussy, humourless Gard McMullen. Explaining that his room was going to be the baby's nursery, she learns that he is a former prison officer. 'Well, you'll be used to a small room.'

Quigley sets to work on McMullen and makes overtures about a bit of 'co-operation'. As the monster truck rumbles through the village, causing terror and panic, Quigley plies McMullen with whisky and offers him the use of a car. Foley is very pleased with McMullen's work and expresses concern that Ambrose and Quigley are related. There could be a conflict of interests, he suggests. He indicates that McMullen might even stay on, with Ambrose moving to an inner-city posting. Niamh and Ambrose are horrified.

Gard McMullen takes steps to halt Quigley's massive lorry.

Father Clifford searches for the mother of the abandoned baby and suspicion falls on teenager Grainne Quinn. While she shuns Father Clifford's offer of help, her brother Roy eventually relents and admits to having helped Grainne with the baby. Father Mac is becoming increasingly uncomfortable about his curate's talk. 'Can I give this talk?' demands Father Clifford. 'Only if it corresponds fully with the teachings of the Church,' answers Father Mac. 'Don't worry, Father,' counters Father Clifford sarcastically, 'I won't be handing out condoms at the door.'

Wise to Quigley's machinations, McMullen impounds the lorry. Realising that he has to get rid of the new man, Quigley hatches a plot by offering McMullen somewhere to live. On the evening of the 'sex talk', McMullen muscles in on proceedings to deliver his own lecture on road safety. Foley is there to see it and Quigley arranges for details of McMullen's bribes — the house, the car and the video — to be discussed right under the Superintendent's nose. Foley realises McMullen is no different and sends him packing. Deliberately given the wrong time by Dr Ryan, Father Mac arrives just too late to hear Father Clifford's talk.

Grainne is rushed to hospital. Her father arrives from Dublin and the whole business comes out into the open. She was worried about how he would react, but he is just delighted that his daughter and grandson are safe. Grainne decides to keep the baby.

Quigley is preening himself over McMullen's departure. He is relieved that Ambrose is back in charge — until Ambrose tells him that he won't let him use the truck, either.

Someone To Watch Over Me

writer: Niall Leonard

director: Dermot Boyd

transmission date: 2 February 1997

Kathleen's cousin Nora, an attractive and flirtatious middle-aged woman, is taken on as housekeeper by Quigley. Her arrival upsets Niamh who not only feels that her territory has been invaded, but also resents Nora's criticism of her housekeeping standards, sparked by the discovery of cobwebs in the kitchen. 'Her and her cobwebs,' complains Niamh to Assumpta. 'You'd think it was Dracula's castle, the way she went on.' But while Niamh thinks that Nora's nothing more than a gold-digger, Quigley can hardly believe his luck. Nora waits on him hand and foot – even bringing him breakfast in bed – and makes it clear that she finds him attractive. Nora has been staying with Kathleen, but Quigley suggests that it would be more convenient all round if she were to move in with him.

Kathleen introduces Quigley to her cousin Nora, the housekeeper from hell.

Quigley plans adding a snooker room to his home, but when Nora sees the untidy pile of building materials, she orders Liam and Donal to dispose of it. Spotting a money-making opportunity, they offer to build Siobhan a porch with the stuff. Quigley is livid, but Nora manages to calm him down.

Naturally enough, Niamh is still upset over losing the baby and is taking out her frustration on the hapless Ambrose, who has feelings of his own, but nobody seems to notice. Aware that the pair seem to be avoiding each other, Father Clifford tries to comfort Niamh who concedes that 'marriage means you should be miserable together'.

Brendan acquires ten new pupils at his school when another school closes down. The new intake are rowdy and uncontrollable, none more so than ten-year-old 'Genghis' Con O'Neill. Genghis and his gang have already turned round every signpost in the village before they skip school and run amok at Kathleen's shop. The redoubtable Kathleen locks them in the storeroom and summons Ambrose, but when he tries to bring them out, he is pelted with flour and eggs. Father Clifford offers to go in, but Ambrose, having watched too many episodes of *NYPD Blue*, fears a hostage situation. Amid all the mayhem, Niamh turns up, calmly marches into the storeroom and makes the boys come out and apologise to Kathleen. Brendan is so impressed that he asks her to help out at the school.

Siobhan registers her displeasure at Liam and Donal's handiwork.

Father Clifford and Assumpta have a late night drink where they discuss everyone else's problems, but when the subject turns to themselves, he makes his excuses and leaves.

The increasingly domineering Nora tells Quigley off for coming home late one night and letting his dinner spoil. Although he has already had dinner, he feels obliged to eat what Nora has cooked for him, slipping the potatoes into his pocket while her back is turned. But when she starts throwing away his favourite clothes and announces that she will move in – on condition that she can have Niamh's old room – he realises things are getting out of hand. 'She's taken over my life – she's like a woman possessed,' he laments. And it emerges that both of her previous husbands had died – she is obviously on the lookout for number three.

The situation calls for drastic action. Quigley invites Father Mac round for a sauna. Nora enters the sauna and, seeing a towelled figure with his face covered, thinks it is Quigley, and puts her hand on his leg. When Father Mac reveals his true identity, both are mortified, even more so since the scene was witnessed by Niamh. Fearing widespread gossip, Father Mac orders Quigley to get rid of Nora. He is only too happy to oblige.

The grand unveiling of Siobhan's porch is a disaster – Liam and Donal hadn't left any room for her front door to open. She tells them to demolish their handiwork.

Only Skin Deep

writer: Jo O'Keefe

director: Dermot Boyd

transmission date: 9 February 1997

The village is preparing for its annual festival, the highlight of which promises to be a beauty contest to find the 'Lily of Ballykissangel'. Quigley is arranging the contest and has even come up with a sponsor, a bottled spring water company called Babbling Brook. As the regulars discuss the contest in the pub, Eamonn walks in with a stunningly beautiful young woman whom he introduces as Naomi, his niece from Dublin. The men flock around her like bees to a honeypot, much to the irritation of the women. 'The last time I saw legs like that, they were hanging from a nest,' comments Niamh caustically. Kathleen is none too impressed with the newcomer, either. When Naomi calls at her shop and asks for some cream to remove hair from legs, Kathleen informs her: 'There's no call for that sort of thing around here.'

There is a distinct chill in the air between Father Clifford and Assumpta. She is still angry because he walked out on her the other night – she says he's supposed to be her friend, yet he listens to everyone except her. Father Clifford has another problem to deal with – Eamonn's ailing pigs. Eamonn thinks they're on their last trotters and wants to know the Church's views on pigs when they pass on. Father Clifford offers to call round and say a few prayers for them. During her visits to Eamonn's farm to tend to his pigs, Siobhan becomes increasingly suspicious about Naomi, particularly when Kathleen tells her that Eamonn has not spoken to his sister in years.

At school, Niamh catches 'Genghis' stealing her purse. She hauls him off to Ambrose, who finds that he and the boy share a common interest in playing the fiddle. 'Genghis' agrees to play at the festival.

Siobhan forces Eamonn to tell the truth about Naomi. She is in fact no relation, but has been brought into the village by Quigley, specifically for the beauty contest, the rules stipulating that all contestants must be local girls. Her real name is Finnoula McMichael. Quigley has promised to arrange for her to win the contest and therefore launch her modelling career, in return for getting a major building contract off her father Dessy, owner of a Dublin shipping firm.

NAOMI (discussing the Ballykissangel Festival): *It's always amusing to see these little country traditions.*

ASSUMPTA: *Oh yeah, you'll love it. We still burn witches at the stake.*

In Fitzgerald's, Siobhan keeps the information to herself but argues against the contest. Quigley reacts by insulting her – what could she possibly know about beauty contests? Later, Brendan calls by to console her and finds her drunk and upset. She misinterprets his attempts at reassurance and jumps on him. Waking up the next morning and finding himself in her bed, he is worried that she might want a deep and meaningful relationship with him. Father Clifford advises him to be honest with her but the misunderstanding deepens when Siobhan finds a bunch of flowers on her doorstep (a peace offering from Quigley) and assumes they are from Brendan.

At the festival, Siobhan tells Assumpta all about the rigging of the beauty contest and the two are about to expose Naomi as a fraud when the results are announced. Naomi/Finnoula hasn't won – the prize goes to Deidre, a local girl. Dessy McMichael is furious with Quigley. Brendan finally plucks up the courage to talk to Siobhan, but she beats him to it. She doesn't want a relationship either.

Ambrose discovers the good side of 'Genghis' Con O'Neill.

Money, Money, Money

writer: Rio Fanning

director: Dermot Boyd

transmission date: 16 February 1997

A fire at Kathleen's house causes considerable consternation among the villagers, especially when they learn that she is not insured. While she is packed off to her sister's, they hold a collection so that the house can be repaired by the time she returns. Everyone digs deep, Father Clifford included, this despite the fact that Father Mac is also pressuring him for money towards the upkeep of the parish church. Being Father Mac, it is not so much a request as a command.

> QUIGLEY: *Kathleen alright?*
>
> FATHER CLIFFORD: *Physically, yeah, but she's very shocked.*
>
> QUIGLEY: *Where is she?*
>
> FATHER CLIFFORD: *She's in the pub with Assumpta.*
>
> QUIGLEY: *No wonder she's shocked.*

Quigley bumps into an old acquaintance, Mossy Phelan, who lets him in on a betting scam he is operating. Black Dazzler, the favourite in a greyhound race, is being switched for a ringer and Mossy and his associates are plunging their cash on the second favourite, Tarbert Warrior. The lure of investing £4,000 to win £50,000 proves irresistible to Quigley.

The collection for Kathleen has only raised £200 so Siobhan suggests betting the money on a dead cert – a greyhound called Black Dazzler. When Quigley hears about this, he tells Niamh to make sure the money is put on Tarbert Warrior instead. At confession, Niamh hints to Father Clifford that the race has been fixed. Thus when the time comes to place the bets, Father Clifford says he has inside information and urges that the money go on Tarbert Warrior. He can only watch in dismay as Black Dazzler romps home. Quigley is none too thrilled either. Not surprisingly, Mossy Phelan has made himself scarce.

Desperate to recoup their losses, the villagers decide to stage a poker tournament at Fitzgerald's, placing their faith in Siobhan's expertise at cards. Phelan reappears, partly to gloat at Quigley. The sting had been an act of revenge, Quigley having once cheated him out of £1,000. Phelan, too, enters the tournament, which

NIAMH: *Go on out and direct traffic or something.*

AMBROSE: *There's no traffic at this hour of the morning.*

NIAMH: *Find some.*

develops into a showdown between him and Siobhan. Soon there is £1,900 on the table but Siobhan, unable to cover it, faces defeat until Quigley throws in a cheque. Phelan objects, but Father Clifford, as referee, rules that the cheque is acceptable. Siobhan wins, whereupon an angry Phelan challenges Quigley to bet the £1,000 on a straight deal. Father Clifford deals and Phelan loses out again.

Kathleen returns to Ballykissangel to be greeted by her newly refurbished home. When she asks where the money came from, they tell her it was a collection. Some things are better kept secret.

Mossy Phelan watches as Quigley goes to the dogs.

Chinese Whispers

writer: Rio Fanning

director: Dermot Boyd

transmission date: 23 February 1997

The mysterious Tom and Jerry spread fear through the entire community.

A burst water tank seems to be the last straw for Assumpta. She tells Niamh that she is fed up with life in BallyK and is considering an offer from a friend to run a wine bar in Dublin. Troubles too, for Quigley, who arrives home to find that his safe has been burgled. £2,000 is missing, along with his account books. He refuses to notify the police, principally because the books are dodgy. His accountant, Cathal, wonders whether the break-in is the work of the Revenue, a suggestion which becomes more credible with the sighting of two mysterious strangers, Tom and Jerry, in the village. Only Ambrose knows who they are, but he isn't letting on.

As rumours about the Revenue men spread, the villagers are thrown into a state of panic. Eamonn dashes out of the pub and is seen burying his car under a pile of hay. Apparently he has been putting agricultural diesel in his car and is terrified that the Revenue are after him. Even the upright Kathleen worries that she might have made a mistake with her books and contemplates going on the run. Father Mac also has cause for concern and asks Father Clifford to cover for him, but the latter refuses initially.

Siobhan is offered the chance of becoming a Peace Commissioner by businessman Sean Dooley, an old enemy of Quigley's. For his part, Quigley receives a ransom demand for his stolen books. He decides to pay the £1,000 which he deposits by a well. The money is collected and the books are left under a pew in St Joseph's.

Father Clifford asks Assumpta whether the rumours about her leaving are true. Although she says that nothing is definite, he is hurt that she didn't talk to him about it. Eventually the fear being caused by the two mystery men gets to him and he agrees to store an illegal load of duty free lager belonging to Assumpta.

Quigley's burglar turns out to be a vengeful Mossy Phelan and nothing to do with the Revenue. Furthermore, Tom and Jerry are not from the Revenue, either – they're from the Bureau of Fraud Investigation and their target is Sean Dooley, wanted for bribery, corruption and tax evasion. The folk of Ballykissangel can breathe easily at last. And Niamh has greater cause for celebration than most – she is pregnant again.

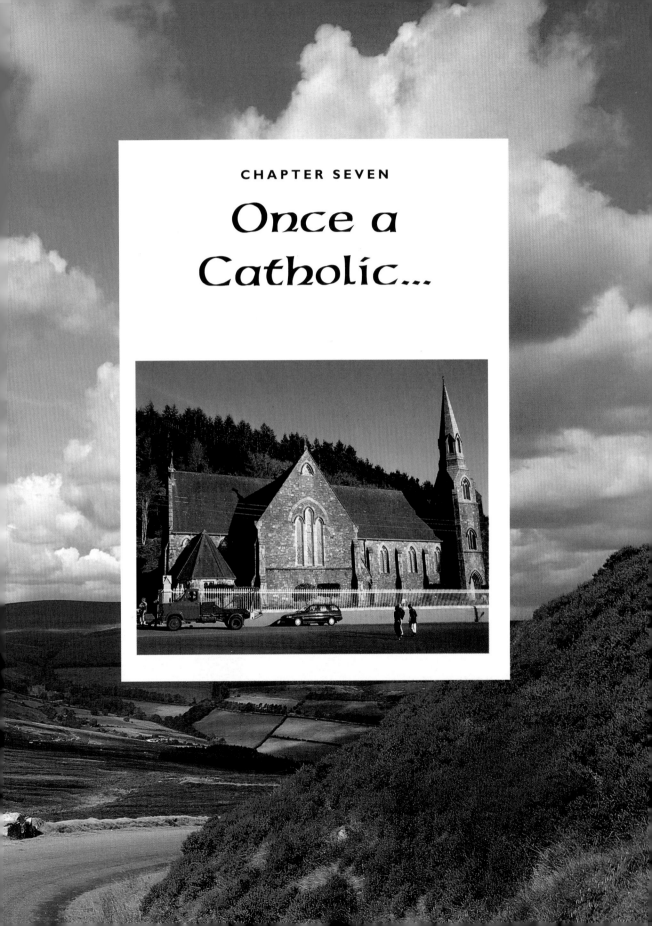

CHAPTER SEVEN

Once a Catholic...

O ver recent years, the Church in Ireland has been going through troubled times. There have been allegations of priests having sex with young boys and affairs with women. The scandal has eroded the traditional trust which most of the Irish people felt towards the priesthood.

The situation called for a knight in shining armour — a high-profile priest of unblemished character who could restore faith in the Church. Enter, by pure chance, Father Peter Clifford.

'Father Clifford is a wonderful role model,' says Father Dan Breen, Avoca's colourful parish priest. 'He comes over as a likeable, caring young man who is genuinely concerned for the welfare of his community. He's decent, approachable and not at all pious — he's not one of those "Holy Joe" priests. And there's none of that bile and ranting and raving that you get from some of the clergy. Above all, he hasn't jumped into bed with the woman who runs the bar.'

Like many real-life priests, Father Clifford is not averse to enjoying a drink at the bar.

Now sixty-seven, Father Breen has been a priest for fifty years. His church, St Mary and Patrick's, doubles as St Joseph's in the series. 'When the producers first asked me for permission to film in the church, I wasn't sure. But when I read the scripts and saw they were harmless, I said OK. I didn't even consult my bishop. It was at the time that the paedophile scandal was breaking, so I think he had more important things to deal with.

'To be honest, I didn't think the programme would get off the ground but I'm delighted that it has, because it does nothing but good for the Church. Some of the Irish people aren't mad about it, but I think that's because in Ireland these days, it's fashionable to be abusive towards priests. *Ballykissangel* isn't, but that could be because it's made by an English company. If the same series had been made in Ireland, it would probably have been very anti-clergy.

'The British people are fed up with violence on their screens, and that's why *Ballykissangel* is such a refreshing change. These days if you see a couple together on TV, you don't know whether they're making love or fighting. But there's none of that in *Ballykissangel*. It's like *Snow White*.

'Both Father Clifford and Father Mac are more rational than many real priests I've met. Father Mac is crafty but, believe me, in real life they're even cuter than that. I'm not sure that a young priest would be as involved in the day-to-day affairs of the village as much as Father Clifford is, but I like to see him go into the bar and have a real drink. That's what I do.'

Having given permission to film, Father Breen likes to keep out of the way and let the crew get on with it. 'If they want to film in the church all day, I simply move out and say Mass in my house. There's plenty of room there. My only real involvement has been to advise the costume department on what clothes the actors should wear. Sure, I chat to the actors in the street if I see them. I know Niall Toibin – I've played golf with him – and I'll maybe joke with Stephen Tompkinson that there's two funerals tonight, but not to worry, I'll handle them!

'As Avoca's fame has spread, we get a lot more visitors to the church. I've got four or five visitors' books filled with names from England. For every one candle we used to have in the church, there are now 1,000 – we almost need the Fire Brigade on stand-by! When I showed my books to my accountant, he thought there had to be some mistake because of the vast number of shrine candles I'd ordered. I pointed out that things had changed a bit since *Ballykissangel* came to town.'

Despite the occupation of its central character, religion is not an overpowering factor in *Ballykissangel*. It does not set out to be controversial but neither does it duck contemporary problems. Producer Chris Griffin says: 'We haven't tried to pull any punches with religion and we've been on the edge of dealing with a few contentious issues, such as euthanasia and single mothers. The only letters of complaint we've had followed the episode where Liam and Donal erected the statue of the Madonna of the Motherlode. Even then, it was only a few letters, but I was conscious of it. So we've tried to redress the situation in episode two of the new series when there's a similar little miracle, again with Liam and Donal up to no good, but this time they get a real dressing-down from Father Clifford who refers back to the first time, saying "I let that one go and I realise I shouldn't have." But *Ballykissangel* isn't about raising big issues regarding religion in Ireland.'

Deborah Jones, editor of the *Catholic Herald,* is another fan of *Ballykissangel.* 'I enjoy it very much and I think it presents a very attractive image of the Church. I hope that it is helping to restore the credibility of the Church as part of the fabric of life and make people realise that there are good and bad priests, just the same as there are good and bad people in other professions or vocations. I like the characters too, especially the fact that the heroine is not a Church-going Catholic. I know a number of priests like Father Mac, and I wish I knew more like Father Clifford…'

Stephen Tompkinson can see why his character is viewed as a good role model. 'Father Clifford is rock solid in his faith and vocation. He does want to help people, but not in the way that he's been brought up with. He has seen priests as black and white, if you like, but wants to encourage people to explore the grey areas, to think for themselves, to find the right solutions. He's trying to encourage and appeal to a new generation, otherwise the Church will die. It's something I think the Church needs to do – to address problems for a modern generation and urge people to stay within the Church.'

Stephen is full of admiration for the priests he has encountered. 'All the priests that I grew up around were trying to do their best for the community they worked in.' He has also been touched by the letters of support he has received from the clergy. 'I've had very encouraging letters from priests, and not just Roman Catholic ones, who say they believe in my portrayal and think *Ballykissangel* puts across the sort of struggles the clergy can have with their faith. I think they're pleased that their vocation isn't pilloried. In most programmes, the vicar or priest has been seen as a buffoon – from Derek Nimmo days – and that has been stamped in people's minds. But *Ballykissangel* and *The Vicar of Dibley,* in which Dawn French is about the only sane person in the village, show the clergy in a different light.

'Priests say that *Ballykissangel* is very believable, that it's showing all aspects of daily life and not glamorising anything, because being a priest is not a very glamorous existence. Above all, they like the way it shows Peter as a human being. Their basic message seems to be "keep up the good work", which I think is fantastic. Praise indeed.'

OPPOSITE *As in any Irish community, the church is a strong focal point of life in Ballykissangel.*

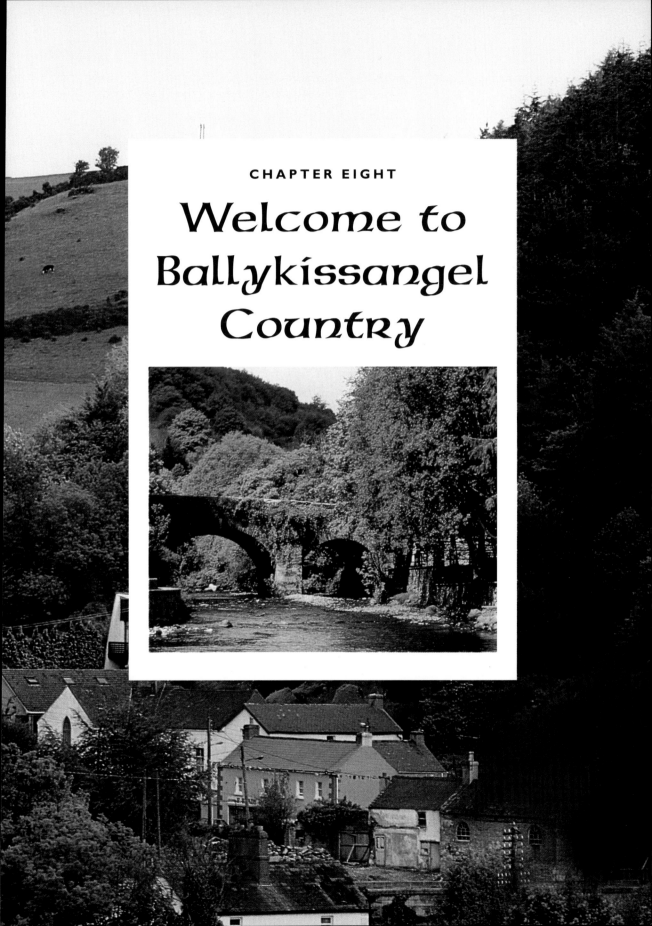

CHAPTER EIGHT

Welcome to Ballykissangel Country

'There is not in this wide world a valley so sweet

As the vale in whose bosom the bright waters meet.

Oh! The last rays of feeling and life must depart

Ere the bloom of that valley shall fade from my heart.'

THOMAS MOORE (1779–1852)

It was in 1807 that Thomas Moore sat beneath a riverside tree in the Vale of Avoca and wrote his song 'The Meeting of the Waters', dedicated to the place of that name where the Avonbeg and Avonmore rivers come together to form the Avoca River. The rivers meet three miles north of the small settlement of Avoca, a village now better known to millions across the world as Ballykissangel.

The arrival of the television cameras and the ensuing fame have transformed the village. Where once there was high unemployment and a general air of resignation, now there is a bustling tourist industry as 400,000 visitors a year descend upon the area in search of the locations for their favourite TV series. *Songs of Praise* has been broadcast from the village church and the *Holiday* programme has featured the area as a travel destination. The upsurge of interest has resulted in a couple of hotels adding extensions to cope with the extra demand for rooms. Peter Caffrey, who plays Padraig in the show, is stunned by the transition. 'When we first went to Avoca, there was over sixty-five per cent unemployment, and the whole village was just dull grey stone. They didn't know what to make of us. But now the village is bright and there are coaches and car parks everywhere. The place is booming.'

'It's amazing,' muses Stephen Tompkinson. 'We've had as many as twenty coachloads a day passing through Avoca while we have been filming there, plus all the people in cars. Sometimes it's like a meeting of the United Nations with visitors from all four home countries, Belgians, Dutch, Canadians, Maltese, New Zealanders and Australians. I keep getting molested by groups of old ladies. I've been swamped a couple of times by coachloads of female tourists who grab various parts of my anatomy while photos are being taken. It's like a Chippendales' concert!

'Being in Avoca is the most special time for me. The tourists have always been very good about letting us get on with filming and because the programme has such a warmth to it, people's reactions to it are very genuine and affectionate. I'll happily sit out all day and sign postcards. Writers' cramp does set in after a while but people have travelled a long way and they're not asking for much.'

Stephen is still coming to terms with the reaction he gets when wearing his dog collar and robes. 'I'm not accustomed to being treated with such reverence – it's a lot to live up to. I get odd looks walking into a country pub in a dog collar.

People stop swearing and start speaking in whispers. When they saw me hugging a make-up lady on set, I'm sure they thought they had another priest scandal on their hands.'

Of course, some people just want to take the mickey. 'It was all right, the first few pleading with me to hear their confession, but the joke can wear a bit thin…'

Jim McCabe of the Avoca Tourist Board confirms: 'There's no doubt about it – the village was in decline. But even before *Ballykissangel,* steps were being taken to remedy matters. Two years before the film crew came, the Vale of Avoca Development Association was formed to refurbish the village, and *Ballykissangel* has accelerated that process. Now we get tourists from all over the world. The only problem is that they tend to be part of whistle-stop tours which means they don't actually stay in the region. And that's a shame because there's excellent accommodation locally. So now we've put together our own brochure to sell the Vale of Avoca to holidaymakers.

'The people of Avoca are delighted and proud that their village was chosen for the series, and much of that is down to the way in which the cast and crew have gone out of their way to be friendly. They seem only too happy to sign autographs

The Meeting of the Waters.

and pose for photographs. And the show itself has that wonderful feelgood factor. It's Ireland as it is and also as you want it to be. I must confess when we first heard the name "Ballykissangel", we thought it sounded too 'Oirish', but the show gets away with it because it is witty. Mind you, if the standards should ever slip – even for just one episode – the villagers will be the first to complain.'

As you walk along the main street of Avoca (population around 850), there are numerous reminders of the village's alter-ego. Outside the tea shop that doubles as the show's post office is a sign urging visitors to 'Eat in Ballykissangel Post Office'. A few doors further along, piped Irish music draws visitors into Avoca Gifts where fans can buy *Ballykissangel* caps, T-shirts, tea towels, key rings, erasers, rulers, CDs, framed photographs of Fitzgerald's, postcards of Fitzgerald's and fudge. There are even rumours of a Ballykissangel cheese.

Avoca Gifts is overseen by Tony Kelly, who also owns the village's major tourist attraction – Fitzgerald's. It was formerly known as the Fountain Bar, but visitors were so disappointed at not being able to take souvenir photographs of the exterior of their favourite pub that he obtained permission from the BBC to change the name to Fitzgerald's. Now a non-stop stream of photographers stand in the middle of the road, oblivious to traffic, so that they can take pictures of friends and family beneath the Fitzgerald's sign. Whereas in many rural villages, the essential item of equipment is a rucksack, in Avoca it is a camcorder.

Inside it is equally busy with Tony Kelly cheerfully attending to his customers' every need. Photos of Stephen Tompkinson and Dervla Kirwan adorn the bar and T-shirts announcing 'I Had a Pint at Fitzgerald's' sell at £7.99 a time.

'*Ballykissangel* has been a tremendous boost for business,' says Tony Kelly. 'It has put Avoca on the map. The pub used to be quiet during the day but now it is busy all the time. Before, I only did a bit of food but now I do a lot more because that's what the visitors want.

'When I first heard about this proposed series, I thought it was probably a Channel 4 documentary, but then I realised it was more than that. And when I saw names like Dervla Kirwan and Tony Doyle, I knew it would be quality, so I had no qualms about helping out. The filming has only ever been of actors walking through the door so it's not too disruptive. It's a question of mutual cooperation. The crew often film early in the morning, so I'll open up a bit later.

'It's every businessman's dream for something like this to happen and you have to move fast to make the most of it. My girlfriend, Paula Fitzpatrick, runs the gift shop and recently I bought the supermarket next door to the pub and turned it into an ice cream parlour and craft shop. I suppose I'm the local Brian Quigley…but with scruples. And when tourists want to take photos of me, I have to admit it's good for the ego.'

He is quick to point out that the gift shop doesn't only sell *Ballykissangel* merchandise. 'Sure, the T-shirts do well, but the best sellers of all are leprechauns.'

At one point the enterprising Tony Kelly was charging £2 a head for tourists to have their photos taken alongside a full-sized cardboard cut-out of Stephen Tompkinson. 'You wouldn't have minded,' says Stephen, 'but it wasn't even my body. It was my head stuck on to someone shorter and plumper!'

Across the main street at Hendley's, owner Des Hendley reports a thirty per cent increase in trade since *Ballykissangel*. 'The show has been of great benefit to local businesses. We usually sell groceries, sweets and newspapers, but we've had to expand our range of postcards of the village as well as start stocking *Ballykissangel* caps, pens and T-shirts, because that's what the tourists want. Most of them take photos of the outside of the shop, but in the window I've got a nice photo of the cast and crew and I've had numerous requests for copies of that.'

Des, who has run the shop for over thirty years, even re-wrote the scripts. He explains: 'Kathleen was originally going to be called Conor but I said it was daft to keep taking my sign down and putting up a new one every time they wanted to film, so they changed her surname to Hendley. It made sense all round – and it certainly hasn't harmed my takings!'

Visitors from all over the world gather on a daily basis outside Fitzgerald's.

'When I first heard that there were plans to film a major new television series in the village, I thought it was a con job. But when we had the big meeting, I realised it was for real. Everyone was very straight and honest with us and, although I had a few initial qualms about letting them film in the shop, I talked it over with my family and we decided to give it the go-ahead.

'I think my shop was chosen because of the steps leading up to it – I suppose it creates a sense of the stage. We came to a mutual arrangement regarding filming and while they like to film in the shop by day, it is usually in my slacker times. I have to close the shop during filming, but my customers understand. Besides, I've got a chip shop attached, so we open that instead for the sale of newspapers and so on.

'Everyone on the production has been really helpful. The cast are extremely approachable – I often chat away to people like Niall Toibin in the shop – and the crew always tidy up after filming. In the episode where the schoolkids created havoc and there was flour and eggs everywhere, the mess was all tidied up long before I got back. Even better was the story where Kathleen's nephew ran a pirate radio station from the storeroom at the back of the shop. The production team were looking for a suitable room to film it and as I was showing them round, they asked, "What's behind that closed door?" I said it was just an old junk room, piled high with old tills, shelving, even a couple of broken TV sets, but they took one look and said it was exactly what they wanted. I'd been meaning to clear out that room for years, but they saved me a job. They took two trailer loads of rubbish to the dump and tidied it all up for me!

'So *Ballykissangel* has been good news for all of us. And of course the villagers love appearing as extras in crowd scenes – not least of all because they get paid for the privilege.'

Established in 1723, clothing manufacturers Avoca Handweavers is Ireland's oldest handweaving mill and one of the major businesses in the vale. Managing director Donald Pratt says: '*Ballykissangel* has been a great boost to business. Although our shops are not souvenir shops and therefore don't stock *Ballykissangel* products, the influx of visitors has been fantastic for the whole of County Wicklow. Above all, the series presents a good image of Ireland and that can only be beneficial.'

With its majestic mountains and lush wooded valleys, County Wicklow is known internationally as 'The Garden of Ireland'. From just south of Dublin, you can drive for an hour down to the Vale of Avoca across a rugged landscape of heather-clad moors, bogs and mountains dotted with tiny corrie lakes, without seeing more than a handful of people or houses.

Southern Wicklow was one of the last strongholds of the Gaelic Irish and to enable the British army to reach the rebels, the Military Road was built, winding south from Glencree on the outskirts of Dublin. It was constructed in the early years of the nineteenth century to deal with the likes of Michael Dwyer who, after the 1798 rising, was able' to remain at liberty in the mountains until 1803. Now a small folk museum, Dwyer's whitewashed thatched cottage still stands in the Glen of Imaal at Derrynamuck. A few miles east of Glencree is the village of Enniskerry, home of the magnificent Powerscourt Estate, the gardens of which are set against the backdrop of the Great Sugar Loaf Mountain. The wilder parts of the estate have long been popular with film crews. Stanley Kubrick's *Barry Lyndon* and Olivier's *Henry V* are among productions shot there. Today Enniskerry itself provides a number of settings for *Ballykissangel*.

One of the most spectacular sections of the Military Road is Sally Gap, a 1,600ft mountain pass. From there, the road drops down into Glenmacnass with its spectacular waterfall. Nearby are Lough Tay (which starred in John Boorman's film *Excalibur*) and Lough Dan, as well as Roundwood, reputed to be the highest village in Ireland. Most of the hinterland of County Wicklow is composed of granite hills, the source of Dublin's River Liffey. A few peaks rise to over 2,000ft with one, Lugnaquillia, attaining a height of 3,039ft, making it Ireland's second highest mountain. At the heart of the Wicklow Mountains is the awe-inspiring Glendalough ('the glen of the two lakes'), a monastic settlement founded in the sixth century by St Kevin and squeezed between two dark lakes and the walls of a deep valley.

Clapper loader Angela Conway prepares Birdy Sweeney for a crowd scene.

The cast of Ballykissangel *pose for a group shot above the Avoca River.*

Head south from Glendalough through the Vale of Cara and you reach the Vale of Avoca and Avondale House which, in 1846, was the birthplace of the great Irish politician Charles Stewart Parnell. Near the Meeting of the Waters is the mottie stone, described variously as the halfway point between Dublin and Wexford, a Stone Age ritual site or a hurling stone of a legendary Celtic warrior. Whatever its origins, visitors are supposed to be able to see the Welsh coast from it on a clear day.

The Wicklow coast stretches from the lively resort of Bray (home of Ardmore Studios) in the north to the bustling port of Arklow in the south where Sir Francis Chichester's round-the-world yacht *Gypsy Moth IV* was built. En route are Kilcoole, the setting for Ireland's leading TV soap opera, *Glenroe*; the yachting centre of Wicklow Town; and the fine sandy beaches of Brittas Bay.

Inland from Arklow is the village of Woodenbridge at the southern end of the Vale of Avoca. With its deep river valleys and densely wooded hills, the vale exudes an atmosphere of peace and tranquility, yet its history revolves around the mining industry. Copper and sulphur had been mined in Avoca since the Bronze Age, but the principal commercial activity began some 250 years ago. The boom years were the 1840s when more than a thousand men were employed in the mining industry. The last mine closed in 1982, but the chimney stacks of the great pumping stations can still be seen today scattered throughout the valley.

The most exciting period in Avoca's history followed the discovery of gold in 1796. In the minor gold rush which ensued, several large nuggets were found, the largest, weighing twenty-two ounces, being made into a snuff box for King George III. Records state that 'so great were the number of peasantry searching and panning that in the short space of six or seven weeks, 2,666 ounces of pure gold were obtained and sold for £10,000.' At today's prices, that would be worth £580,000. By 1801, gold fever had subsided although a few decent-sized nuggets continued to turn up over the next one hundred years, including one which is currently in Dublin's National Museum.

Rumours abound that there is still gold in the area. As recently as a few years ago maps and panning equipment were on sale in the village to would-be prospectors and it was said to be possible to make twenty pounds a week from the remaining deposits. Hardly a fortune but enough to fire the imagination. And amazingly, the episode where Liam and Donal set up their gold-panning operation in the river sparked a new gold rush! 'No sooner had the episode been shown,' says Chris Griffin, 'than there were people down by the river searching for gold. Such is the power of television…'

Father Clifford ponders the meaning of life on the bridge at Avoca.

Unit Lists

UNIT LIST (SERIES 1)

EXECUTIVE PRODUCERS Robert Cooper Tony Garnett
PRODUCER Joy Lale
PRODUCTION EXECUTIVE Kevin Jackson
DIRECTORS Richard Standeven Paul Harrison
SERIES CREATOR Kieran Prendiville
MUSIC Shaun Davey
PRODUCTION MANAGERS Howard Gibbins Mark Huffam
FIRST ASSISTANT DIRECTOR Konrad Jay
PRODUCTION COORDINATOR Breda Walsh
ASSISTANT PRODUCTION COORDINATOR Christina Coyle
PRODUCTION SECRETARY Janette Hamill
UNIT MANAGER/ACTION VEHICLE COORDINATOR Reggie Blain
PRODUCTION TRAINEE Isabel Rofe
PRODUCTION ACCOUNTANT Shruti Shah
ASSISTANT PRODUCTION ACCOUNTANTS Teresa McGrane
    Frank Moiselle
LOCATION MANAGER Constance Harris
ASSISTANT LOCATION MANAGER Adrian McCarthy
SECOND ASSISTANT DIRECTORS Peter Agnew Emma Pounds
THIRD ASSISTANT DIRECTOR Barbara Mulcahy
TRAINEE ASSISTANT DIRECTOR Lizzie Turvey
CASTING DIRECTORS Nuala Moiselle Jane Arnell
PRODUCTION DESIGNER Tom McCullagh
ART DIRECTORS Sarah Hauldren Anna Rackard
ASSISTANT ART DIRECTOR Claire Doherty
PRODUCTION BUYER Jerry Organ
PROP MASTER Peter Hedges
DRESSING PROPS Dave Peters Daragh Lewis
STAND-BY PROPS Pat McKane Owen Monahan
DIRECTORS OF PHOTOGRAPHY Graham Frake John Record
FOCUS PULLERS Jean Paul Seresin Liam Murphy
CLAPPER LOADER Conor Kelly
CAMERA GRIPS Malcolm Huse John Dunne
TRAINEE CAMERA GRIP James Hagan
SOUND RECORDIST Alan O'Duffy
SOUND MIXER Ray Cross
DIGITAL SOUND EDITORS Chris Craver Tim Hodnott
DUBBING MIXER Pip Norton

BOOM OPERATOR Barry O'Sullivan
GAFFER Tony Devlin
BEST BOY Brendan Walls
GENERATOR OPERATOR David Durnay
ELECTRICIAN Richard Nevins
CONSTRUCTION MANAGER Steve Ede
ASSISTANT CONSTRUCTION MANAGER Roland Coyne
MASTER PAINTER Christy O'Shaughnessy
STAND-BY RIGGER Eamonn Kelly
STAND-BY CARPENTER Colm Murnane
STAND-BY PAINTER Tommy O'Shaughnessy
STAND-BY STAGEHAND Noel Keogh
COSTUME DESIGNER Maggie Donnelly
WARDROBE MISTRESS Hazel Webb-Crozier
WARDROBE ASSISTANT Barbara Callaghan
CHIEF MAKE-UP ARTIST Jennifer Hegarty
CHIEF HAIRDRESSERS Dee Corcoran Eileen Doyle
EDITORS Phil Southby Robin Graham-Scott
POST-PRODUCTION SUPERVISOR Phil Brown
SCRIPT EDITOR Roxy Spencer
SCRIPT SUPERVISORS Lindsay Grant Vicky Harrison
UNIT PUBLICIST Gerry Lundberg
SPECIAL EFFECTS Graham Browne Gerry Johnston
STUNT COORDINATOR Philippe Zone
UNIT NURSE Teresa Gantly
LOCATION CATERERS Fitzers
DRIVERS Dan Breen Snr Dan Breen Jnr Tony Mullally
    Sheamus McCabe Patrick Dowling Terence Morrison
    Frank Hudson Bernard Corish Danny Blain Victor Blain
    Wayne Cullen Alan Crozier John Dempsey
WRITERS Kieran Prendiville (Eps one, two, three, six)
    John Forte (four, five)

UNIT LIST (SERIES 2)

EXECUTIVE PRODUCERS Tony Garnett Robert Cooper
PRODUCER Chris Griffin
PRODUCTION EXECUTIVE Kevin Jackson
DIRECTORS Paul Harrison Dermot Boyd
SERIES CREATOR Kieran Prendiville

MUSIC Shaun Davey

PRODUCTION MANAGER Howard Gibbins

FIRST ASSISTANT DIRECTORS David Brown Konrad Jay

PRODUCTION COORDINATOR Carol Moorhead

ASSISTANT PRODUCTION COORDINATOR Rachel Smith

UNIT MANAGER/ACTION VEHICLE COORDINATOR Reggie Blain

PRODUCTION TRAINEE Dermot Whelan

SUPERVISING ACCOUNTANT Shruti Shah

PRODUCTION ACCOUNTANT David Murphy

ACCOUNTS ASSISTANTS Miriam Kane Niall Delaney

LOCATION MANAGER Adrian McCarthy

ASSISTANT LOCATION MANAGER Cathy Pearson

LOCATION TRAINEE Gordon Wycherley

SECOND ASSISTANT DIRECTOR Peter Agnew

THIRD ASSISTANT DIRECTOR Hannah Quinn

TRAINEE ASSISTANT DIRECTOR Sonia Thornton

CASTING DIRECTOR Nuala Moiselle

PRODUCTION DESIGNER David Wilson

ART DIRECTOR Mark Lowry

ASSISTANT ART DIRECTOR Julian King

PRODUCTION BUYER Robert Jones

PROP MASTER Peter Hedges

DRESSING PROPS Daragh Lewis Peter Gallagher

STAND-BY PROP CHARGE-HAND Pat McKane

STAND-BY PROP Owen Monahan

PROP DRIVER Sheamus McCabe

DIRECTORS OF PHOTOGRAPHY John Record Colin Munn

FOCUS PULLERS Conor Kelly Tim Fleming

CLAPPER LOADERS Angela Conway Richie Donnelly
   Darryl Byrne

CAMERA OPERATORS Vic Purcell Seamus Corcoran

CAMERA TRAINEE Edward D'Arcy

STEADICAM OPERATOR Kate Robinson

CAMERA GRIP John Dunne

SCRIPT SUPERVISOR Tasha Chapman

SOUND RECORDIST Alan O'Duffy

DIGITAL SOUND EDITOR Ian Wilkinson

DUBBING MIXERS Hugh Strain Billy Mahoney

BOOM OPERATOR Barry O'Sullivan

GAFFER Tony Devlin

BEST BOY Brendan Walls

GENERATOR OPERATOR Gerry Donnelly

ELECTRICIAN Eugene O'Sullivan

CONSTRUCTION MANAGER Steve Ede

MASTER CARPENTER Roland Coyne

MASTER PAINTER Christy O'Shaughnessy

STAND-BY RIGGER Eamon Kelly

STAND-BY CARPENTER Derek Drew

STAND-BY PAINTER Noel Coughlan

STAND-BY STAGEHAND Noel Keogh

COSTUME DESIGNER Maggie Donnelly

WARDROBE MISTRESS Hazel Webb-Crozier

WARDROBE ASSISTANT Judith Devlin

CHIEF MAKE-UP ARTIST Jennifer Hegarty

MAKE-UP ASSISTANTS Margot Wilson Joni Galvin

CHIEF HAIRDRESSER Eileen Doyle

TRAINEE HAIRDRESSER Una O'Sullivan

EDITORS Robin Graham-Scott Ian Sutherland

POST-PRODUCTION SUPERVISOR Phil Brown

TRAINEE EDITOR Claire Kilroy

SCRIPT EDITOR Maggie Allen

PUBLICIST Kate Bowe

STILLS PHOTOGRAPHERS Pat Redmond Pat Dowling

STUNT COORDINATOR Philippe Zone

UNIT NURSES Olive Drynan Teresa Gantly

LOCATION CATERERS Fitzers

TRANSPORT CAPTAIN Dan Breen Snr

DRIVERS Dan Breen Jnr Tom Sharpe Tony Mullally
   Pat Dowling Terence Morrison Frank Hudson
   Wayne Cullen Danny Blain Victor Blain John McDowell
   Bernard Corish Clark Tracy

WRITERS Kieran Prendiville (Eps one, two)
   John Forte (three, four)
   Niall Leonard (five)
   Jo O'Keefe (six)
   Rio Fanning (seven, eight)

UNIT LIST (SERIES 3)

EXECUTIVE PRODUCERS Brenda Reid Robert Cooper

PRODUCER Chris Griffin

CO-PRODUCERS Conor Harrington Alan Moloney

PRODUCTION EXECUTIVE Kevin Jackson

DIRECTORS Paul Harrison Dermot Boyd Tom Cotter

SERIES CREATOR Kieran Prendiville

MUSIC Shaun Davey

PRODUCTION MANAGER Noëlette Buckley

FIRST ASSISTANT DIRECTORS David Brown Peter Agnew

PRODUCTION COORDINATOR Liza Buckley

ASSISTANT PRODUCTION COORDINATOR Niamh O'Dea

PRODUCTION SECRETARY Oonagh McMorrow

UNIT MANAGER/ACTION VEHICLE COORDINATOR Reggie Blain

LONDON OFFICE COORDINATOR Chris Harries

PRODUCTION TRAINEE Seamus Porter
PRODUCTION ACCOUNTANT Teresa McGrane
ASSISTANT PRODUCTION ACCOUNTANT Niall Delaney
ACCOUNTS ASSISTANT Jean Wainwright
PRODUCTION LAWYERS James Hickey Ruth Hunter
LOCATION MANAGER Luke Johnston
ASSISTANT LOCATION MANAGER Gordon Wycherley
LOCATION TRAINEE Marcus Lynch
SECOND ASSISTANT DIRECTOR John Burns
THIRD ASSISTANT DIRECTORS Dermot Whelan
    Daisy Cummins
TRAINEE ASSISTANT DIRECTORS Ciara O'Sullivan
    Stephen Curran
CASTING DIRECTORS Nuala Moiselle Frank Moiselle
PRODUCTION DESIGNER David Wilson
ART DIRECTOR Mark Lowry
ASSISTANT ART DIRECTOR Siochfradha Kelly
ART DEPARTMENT TRAINEE Ruth Winick
PRODUCTION BUYER Robert Jones
PROP MASTER Daragh Lewis
DRESSING PROPS Peter Gallagher Tony Nicholson
STAND-BY PROP Owen Monahan
CHARGE-HAND PROP Pat McKane
TRAINEE PROP Tony Gallagher
PROP TRUCK DRIVER Sheamus McCabe
DIRECTORS OF PHOTOGRAPHY John Record
    Colin Munn
FOCUS PULLER Conor Kelly
CLAPPER LOADER Angela Conway
CAMERA GRIP John Dunne
CAMERA TRAINEE Edward D'Arcy
SCRIPT SUPERVISORS Tasha Chapman Jean Skinner
    Kathleen Weir
SOUND RECORDIST Alan O'Duffy
BOOM OPERATOR Barry O'Sullivan
SOUND TRAINEES Alan J. Lyons Ernie Gallagher
GAFFER Tony Devlin
BEST BOY Brendan Walls
GENERATOR OPERATOR Gerard Donnelly
ELECTRICIAN Alan Hynes
CONSTRUCTION MANAGER Tom Dowling

SUPERVISING CARPENTER Nick McManus
MASTER PAINTER Tommy Lavelle
CONSTRUCTION CARPENTERS John Lamon
    Darren Crimmins
STAGEHAND John Arkins
STAND-BY RIGGER Eamon Kelly
STAND-BY STAGEHAND Noel Keogh
STAND-BY CARPENTER Mick Kearns
STAND-BY PAINTER Joe Gaynor Snr
CONSTRUCTION BUYER/DRIVER Maurice Thompson
COSTUME DESIGNER Maggie Donnelly
WARDROBE MISTRESS Ann Stokes
WARDROBE ASSISTANT Judith Devlin
CHIEF MAKE-UP ARTIST Margot Wilson
MAKE-UP ASSISTANT Joni Galvin
MAKE-UP TRAINEE Colette Jackson
CHIEF HAIRDRESSER Eileen Doyle
HAIR ASSISTANT Una O'Sullivan
SUPERVISING EDITOR Ian Sutherland
EDITORS Richard Brunskill George Mallen
ASSISTANT EDITOR Claire Kilroy
POST-PRODUCTION SUPERVISOR Phil Brown
SCRIPT EDITOR Ceri Meyrick
PUBLICIST Kate Bowe
STILLS PHOTOGRAPHER Patrick Dowling
STUNT COORDINATOR Philippe Zone
UNIT NURSE Teresa Gantly
LOCATION CATERERS Fitzers
TRANSPORT CAPTAIN Dan Breen Snr
DRIVERS Dan Breen Jnr Tom Sharpe Tony Mullally Victor
    Blain John McDowell Danny Blain George McGlashan
    Frank Hudson Conrad Philips Clark Tracy Wayne
    Cullen Terence Morrison Morrison Hawthorne
WRITERS Barry Devlin (Eps one, two)
    Rio Fanning (three, four, five)
    Niall Leonard (six)
    Felicity Hayes-McCoy (seven)
    Robert Jones (eight)
    Ted Gannon (nine)
    Tim Loane (ten)
    Kieran Prendiville (eleven, twelve)